Bitten by a Hellcat

Felicity Heaton

ETERNAL MATES SERIES

Kissed by a Dark Prince
Claimed by a Demon King
Tempted by a Rogue Prince
Hunted by a Jaguar
Craved by an Alpha
Bitten by a Hellcat
Taken by a Dragon (Coming March 10th 2015)

Find out more at: www.felicityheaton.co.uk

CHAPTER 1

She was a bad little kitty.

One of Hell's own.

And she prowled the nightclub in a way that had every males' eyes glued to her shapely form.

Even his.

Heck, if he was being honest with himself, he wasn't even looking at her as a hunter eyeing potential prey. He was staring at her with a gaze as hungry as the next man's.

Owen leaned his left elbow on the black bar behind him, admiring the way she moved as she danced near the fringes of the Saturday night crowd, every sway of her hips entrancing him. She was beautiful. He had to give her that.

She raised her arms above her head, lifting her dark boned strapless corset and revealing a tantalising flash of toned stomach. Her hips shifted again, the colourful lights of the club reflecting off her tight leather trousers, accenting each dip and gyration she made. Several males nearby, not all of them fae or demon, gawped at her as they danced at a modest distance, every one of them looking as if they might drop dead if she dared to give them an ounce of her attention.

She didn't seem interested in the men present though. She seemed content with dancing alone, lost in the heavy beat of the music, working up a sweat that caused an alluring sheen across her ample cleavage.

Owen didn't feel the pain of the bruises and cuts beneath his black shirt as he watched her. She stole his awareness of the injuries he had sustained on his last job, more effective than any of the painkillers he had taken and the alcohol he had imbibed.

He had come out to Underworld tonight to spend a nice chunk of the fat pay he had received from a small group of rare weak fae after giving the demon who had been terrorising them what he had deserved.

Death.

His father and grandfather were probably turning in their graves because of the changes he had made to the family business.

A Nightingale taking money for services rendered? Shocking.

Owen didn't care that he had turned into more of a mercenary than a were-hunter, ending the family tradition and probably tarnishing their name. The family money had run out shortly after his father's death thanks to his string of marriages, and subsequent divorces.

Owen had had a choice. Go mercenary, or get a paying job. Since he had been raised from birth to be a hunter, the only skills he possessed were fighting and killing, and knowledge of fae and demons. They weren't exactly the sort of qualifications the average office job was looking for, so he had gone mercenary.

Now, he hunted whatever people asked him to hunt, as long as it met his criteria. He refused to hunt fae, demons or shifters who had done nothing wrong. He only took jobs if the enemy involved was a threat to humans or other fae, and even demons sometimes. As far as he could see, he was doing exactly what he would have been doing as a Nightingale, only he was getting paid for it.

The female shifter ran her hands up her body, dragging his focus back to her, and Owen couldn't stop his gaze from tracking them over every lush and tempting curve, especially when she ran them over her breasts and up her neck.

She tangled her fingers in her long dark hair, drawing the damp lengths away from her neck as she closed her eyes, a flicker of bliss crossing her pretty face. The air-conditioning in Underworld was cranked up tonight, but it wasn't enough to combat the heat coming off everyone on the packed dance floor.

It wasn't enough to cool Owen down as he stared at her.

Strong hands clamped down on Owen's shoulders from behind, fingers tipped with short claws pressing through his black shirt, and he stiffened and winced as some of the bruises he had picked up on his last job burned beneath the pressure of the male's grip.

"I'd reconsider if you were thinking of doing something stupid in my club." The deep male voice growled over the thumping rock music, close to his ear, and Owen knew without looking who was behind him on the other side of the bar. Kyter. The big blond shifter owned Underworld and they had a sort of accord. Owen didn't hunt on his turf and Kyter didn't kill him. "I'm not in the mood to see a fellow cat get her tail pulled. I won't be held responsible for how it will end for you."

Kyter released his shoulders.

Owen slowly turned on his stool to face him, his wide eyes meeting the bright golden ones of the jaguar shifter. "I swear, I'm off duty."

Kyter didn't look as if he believed him, but Owen couldn't hold that against him. Kyter and most of the staff at Underworld, and probably most of the non-human patrons, knew what he did for a living and they had every right to be wary around him.

Especially the patrons.

2

Owen guessed that if he took his tablet device out of the bag at the foot of his stool, he would find at least a fifth of them were in his database for some misdemeanour or another.

The sandy-haired male looked as if he might ask him to leave, but then his gaze slid to Owen's right.

Owen looked there and found the female he had been studying bouncing up to the bar, a big smile on her face as she breathed hard. She turned that killer smile on Kyter and Owen felt an undeniable urge to add the shifter to his database. He shot the big jaguar a glare.

Kyter's right eyebrow lifted.

A ripple of heat travelled through Owen and he became aware of the beautiful woman beside him.

Staring at him.

He slowly turned his head towards her as Kyter walked away. Blue eyes met his, turning the ripple of heat into an inferno that blasted through his veins, burning up his blood. A corona of brighter blue fire shone around her dilated pupils as she stared into his eyes, radiating confidence that shook his own.

She was more beautiful than he had thought.

Incredible.

Owen could only stare at her in silence as she looked at him, her long black lashes and dark make-up framing striking blue eyes.

A hellcat.

They were the rarest of the cat shifters and fetched high prices on the black market of Hell.

He had never seen one of her kind, not in all his years as a hunter or during all of the training that had come before them. He doubted that even the hunters who worked for Archangel, the world's leading hunter organisation devoted to protecting the unwitting humans from the secret and often dangerous world of fae and demons, had seen a hellcat.

She turned her cheek to him and flagged a bartender. Owen didn't pay any attention to who served her. He couldn't take his eyes off her as she spoke, her painted red lips moving in a mesmerising symphony, filling him with a fierce need to kiss her.

It was only when she turned back to face him and slid a glass across the black bar top in his direction that he became aware of something else in the club. His pale gaze dropped to the drink she had evidently bought for him.

A shot of Hellfire.

Heck, she was trying to kill him.

Hellfire was a vicious drink brewed by the non-humans, designed to overcome their constitutions and get them drunk.

The female hellcat slid onto the stool beside him, picked up her own shot glass filled to the brim with the black liquid and raised it.

Her wicked smile made it clear that she was testing him. She knew he was mortal and she wanted to see what he would do and whether he could survive downing the potent shot of alcohol. He was up for that challenge. He took a deep breath to steel himself, grabbed his shot glass and lifted it, saluting her.

Owen raised it to his lips.

"Wait." Her light melodic voice stopped him dead and he stared at her, the glass close to his lips, the fumes coming off the liquid singeing his nose.

She flagged the bartender again, her smile turning even more wicked.

When the only female and human bartender working for the club stopped on the other side of the bar, his little hellcat fluttered her eyelashes and dropped a huge hammer on his male pride.

"Can we get a glass of water for when he chokes?"

Owen glared at the bartender, Sherry, warning the blonde not to do as the woman had requested.

Sherry barely managed to hold back her smile and went ahead and kicked him in the balls while he was down by serving up a tall glass of ice-cold water, setting it right down in front of him, her eyes twinkling.

He narrowed his eyes on the water, shoved it away and pinned his gaze back on the female hellcat. She raised her glass, her smile mocking him now. A slow smile spread across his face as he lifted his shot of Hellfire and saluted her again. She didn't know who she was dealing with if she thought this was going to play out the way she wanted it, ending with him coughing up a lung and downing the water.

Owen brought the shot up to his lips, holding her gaze the whole time, staring deep into her eyes. She paused with her glass near her lips, her smile fading as the air between them thickened and sparked with electricity, awareness that zinged through his body. He didn't close his eyes. He kept them locked with hers as he tipped his head back and swallowed the entire contents of the glass.

The liquid burned like the fire it was named after as it slid down his throat and turned his stomach into a pit of churning lava. An inferno swept through him but he held it together, refusing to give the slightest indication of the discomfort he was suffering as his entire body burned and his head turned, his vision swimming slightly from the sudden rise in his blood alcohol level.

He slowly set the glass down, lowered his head, and licked his lips.

Her blue gaze narrowed and she knocked her shot back, slammed the glass down on the black bar top, and stared at him.

Tears lined her long lashes.

Her lips compressed and trembled.

Her right eye developed a vicious tic.

Owen calmly pressed two fingers against the side of the ice-cold glass of water and pushed it along the bar towards her, the condensation on it rolling down and leaving a trail behind it. She glared at the glass, straightened and managed a smile.

He wasn't sure what the point of her entire competition had been, but he had the feeling that he had won and she didn't like it.

She leaned back, brushed her long black hair from her face, and fixed him with her blue eyes and a smile that shook him to his core.

"I don't often see your kind around," she said over the pounding music and leaned closer to him.

Owen fought to stop himself from looking down at her cleavage, casually leaned his left elbow on the bar and smiled at her. "It's not every day I get to see a genuine hellcat. One of the Devil's own."

Born of a land of brimstone and fire where only the strongest survived.

Her kin were the most powerful, and dangerous, shifter species out there. His father would have killed to have met one.

She leaned even closer and ran her right hand down his forearm where it rested on the bar, her light caress heating his skin even through his black shirtsleeve. Her smile turned sultry and a little bit wicked again, making his heart pound harder and his thoughts turn back to kissing her.

"Do you want to see the real me?" Her eyes held him, the fiery blue corona around her pupils burning brighter, making part of him believe she would change right here and show him her cat form if he admitted he wanted to see it, even when the rest of him knew she was teasing. "I can see you're dying to see it."

Flirting.

Definitely flirting with him.

He had enough life experience to know when a woman was flirting with him, but for some reason he hadn't expected it from her. Non-human females were rarely interested in him, especially when they knew what he did for a living as she did. She could have any pick of the males in the club who had been staring at her all night, most of them shifters and fae, and some demons. Males who were still staring at her, and who were shooting him deadly looks. He could almost feel them butchering him in their heads as the female sat with him and he had a feeling he wouldn't survive the night if she did more than just sit beside him and casually flirt.

Owen frowned as he thought back over the hour that had passed since he had first spotted her.

She hadn't looked at any of the men who had tried to dance with her.

She had paid them zero attention.

She hadn't moved into the throng to find a lucky partner more suited to her tastes either.

She had remained at the edge of the dance floor.

Directly in front of him.

Owen stared at her as it struck him hard.

She had been flirting with him the whole time, trying to get his attention and hold it locked on her.

"What if I said yes?" He leaned closer to her, studying her face for a reaction, a tiny flicker of hope or insecurity, something to confirm his suspicions that she had actually singled him out from the moment she had walked into the club.

He had seen her enter, a little out of breath as if she had been running and a little on edge. Her eyes had met his across the club and she had stared at him for a moment before disappearing from view, only to reappear a short time later on the dance floor.

Owen placed his right hand over hers where it rested on his left forearm and looked deep into her striking eyes. "Would you show me just how beautiful you are?"

A blush climbed her cheeks and she took her hand away. "You might not live to tell the tale."

He reached towards her and caught her right hand, bringing it back to him, toying with her slender fingers. Black nails. A hint of what she would look like if she shifted. She was right and he was dying to see her other form. He only had rumours to go on, but if she transformed, she would without a doubt be the most incredible thing he had ever seen.

He raised his eyes back to hers.

Heck, she was already the most incredible thing he had ever seen.

"I can handle myself," he husked and her cheeks darkened further. "I can handle you."

He moved his fingers beneath hers, brushed his thumb over them, and lifted her hand to his lips. He stopped just short, so his mouth hovered bare millimetres from her skin, and she stared at him, her blue eyes wide and entrancing, her lips parted as she breathed harder. The intense sense of anticipation that filled her swirled through him too, cranking him tighter inside and making him itch to drop a kiss on her knuckles, fulfilling both of their desires.

He held her gaze instead and swept his thumb across the backs of her fingers as he spoke, his breath washing over her hand.

"So will you make my wildest dreams come true?"

CHAPTER 2

He was a wicked man.

It thrilled her but Cait hid it behind a smile, concealing how he made her heart flutter and her body heat with only a handful of words and a sultry smile.

She had come into Underworld seeking sanctuary, backed into a corner and in need of a crowded place where the male after her wouldn't dare do anything. He had ambushed her when she had been making her way to the club and she'd had to fight him to get him off her tail. She had barely escaped, twisting free of his clutches as he had attempted to get a wretched restraint on her.

She was no tame kitty and she didn't want a collar, and that was exactly what the male hellcat intended to give to her.

Plenty of fiery females of her race had met their end in a piece of steel and leather, reinforced by magic to subdue the wearer and place them under the control of another.

Their 'mate'.

That wasn't the life for Cait, and if she had to run forever, she would keep on running until she met her true mate, the one fated for her.

She glanced across the heaving nightclub towards the shadowy corner where the big dark-haired male lurked. She could feel his eyes on her and she refused to let him fluster her. She was safe here. He couldn't do anything in such a public place except glare at her.

If he were foolish enough to try, the staff would step in to protect her.

The owner in particular would. Kyter had always been good to her whenever she had braved leaving Hell to visit his club. He would keep the big male away from her.

Maybe the man opposite her would too.

There was something about him that drew her to him. He felt dangerous for a mortal, an edge of darkness lacing his scent, and power. There was a sense of menace in his looks too, in the intensity of his fierce gaze. He was right and he was a man who could handle himself, despite the fact he was mortal. That sensation of danger had drawn her gaze to him the second she had walked into the club and the sight of him had stopped her in her tracks.

He was handsome, an example of male perfection with his high cheekbones and defined jaw that framed a straight nose, sensual bowed lips and eyes that shone with intelligence and confidence, and a glimmer of darkness. His short dark hair, black jeans and shirt were a contrast to the paleness of those eyes that made them stand out even more.

They were green.

She had been itching to know their colour since setting eyes on him. With every change of song, she had come close to leaving the dance floor and approaching him, barely stopping herself and then finding the strength to resist when the next tune began.

She had given up her fight against his dark allure when Kyter had spoken to him and she had realised that the male knew the big jaguar, and had heard their conversation. One of the perks of being a hellcat. She could tune out any noise in order to focus on one in particular. She had snooped, and what she had heard had been enough to pique her interest and shatter her weakening will to resist approaching him.

A hunter.

His pale green eyes darted between hers and she could sense his eagerness as he held her hand close to his lips, on the verge of kissing it. Cait wanted to push her hand forwards and make him do it, as eager for him to kiss it as he was.

She played it cool instead.

"I'm not sure I should promise to make your wildest dreams come true when I don't even know your name." She smiled and he echoed it, his profane lips curving wickedly again.

For a mortal, this male was dangerous beyond all expectation, but she didn't mean it in the violence and strength sense this time. He was dangerous on another, intimate level. He wreaked havoc on her body and her control, every smile or glance pushing her closer to the edge and making her want to give up the charade they were playing and kiss him.

He wanted her.

She could see it in his eyes and feel it in the way he touched her, his light caress making her burn inside.

She wanted him too.

The game they played was pointless and stupid. Dancing around their mutual desire only made them have to wait longer to get what they wanted.

A taste of each other.

She had waited too long as it was, passing years without a male's touch, leading a solitary life in Hell. She had grown bored of the hunt and the thrill at the end of it almost a century ago, craving something more than brief trysts with males, even when she pretended that hunger didn't exist. She had decided long ago that she would spend her life free of the complications of relationships and she had stuck to that plan for countless centuries.

That vow had shattered the moment her gaze had met his across the nightclub.

He had awakened desire in her again, passion that had been dormant and now felt as if it would consume her, need that burned so fiercely she feared it might rage out of control if she didn't find a release for it soon. Just a glimmer of satisfaction.

A single kiss would do.

For now.

She twisted her hand in his, reversing their positions, and brought his hand to her lips. Her eyes held his as she pressed a kiss to it and breathed him in, his rich scent of spice and fire, and something else branding itself on her senses. What secret did he hold that gave him the strength to fight demons and powerful fae and survive? Whatever it was, it was in his blood, lacing his scent, making it dark and alluring.

His pale green eyes narrowed on her lips where they pressed against his callused large hand.

"Owen," he muttered and then his voice gained strength as he straightened and lifted his eyes to hers. He looked as if he was gauging her again, studying her reactions. "Owen Nightingale."

Cait could see why he had been watching her closely now, eyeing her like the hunter he was, no doubt putting everything about her to memory so he could note it all down later.

Including how she reacted to hearing that he was a member of the most illustrious hunter family to have ever existed.

Did he think she would turn tail and run on hearing that he was a Nightingale?

She wasn't afraid. She was impressed. The perfect and handsome Owen had just become a shade more perfect for her.

"I'm Cait, with a C." She twisted their hands again and shook his.

He raised a dark eyebrow. "Like Cat, with an I?"

She shrugged and nodded. "My parents thought they were being cute."

Owen looked her over, a leisurely raking of his eyes from her head to her toes that set her on fire.

His expression gave nothing away, not a single thought or feeling.

"Maybe they thought you were cute and deserved a cute name to match."

Gods, she wanted to ask what he thought but bit her tongue to stop herself. "Most people don't think hellcats are cute."

"I'm not most people." That flicker of wickedness was back in his eyes as he gave her another once over. "But I can't really judge whether you're cute or not since I've never seen a hellcat in their true form."

Cait narrowed her gaze on him and shot him a sultry smile of her own. "I know you're dying to see me in just my fur."

He looked as if he might blush, but rallied and fixed her with hungry eyes that left her in zero doubt of his desire. "I wouldn't say no to seeing you naked."

She flushed all over, hot from head to toe at just the thought of getting naked with him. She leaned closer, reached her right hand out, and stroked her fingers down his chest. It was as hard as steel beneath the soft material of his black shirt. She heated further, burning hotter as she raced to imagine just how good he would look naked, that honed body on display for her hungry gaze to devour.

Cait wrestled for control over herself and won, refusing to let him fluster her when she was trying to fluster him.

She tilted her head to one side and looked deep into his piercing green eyes. "What's your view on interspecies relationships? You must like tangling with other species since you're a hunter."

His sensual lips quirked into another smile. "I've tangled with many species… but never with a hellcat."

"No?" Cait leaned closer, feeling a little breathless as she narrowed the distance between them. "You don't know what you're missing."

Owen mirrored her, moving closer, his heat washing over her and his heart thumping like a drum in her head, a beat hers tried to match.

"I think I do know." He raked his dark gaze over her again and scrubbed a hand down over his mouth. "But I wouldn't say no to finding out."

Her heart fluttered again and she wriggled on her seat, tempted to take him up on that offer. She needed to do some business with him first though. Pleasure could come later.

He was a Nightingale. *The* Nightingale. The infamous Owen. Last hunter of his bloodline.

Her best shot at survival.

"I have an offer you can't resist." She slipped her fingers between the buttons of his black shirt and drew him closer still. "I need you to do a job for me."

A brief flicker of disappointment crossed his handsome face before his expression hardened, turning too business-like for her. She hadn't meant to douse the fire that had been burning between them, not completely. She had only meant to dial it back a few degrees, from inferno to wildfire, for as long as it took to convince him to take a job from her.

Cait rubbed the material of his shirt between her fingers and thumb, her eyes holding his, even when she accidentally on purpose shifted her hand forwards an inch, bringing the backs of her fingers into contact with his bare chest beneath his shirt. His eyes instantly darkened again, the fire flaring back into life in them.

Just the way she liked it.

She was beginning to crave that way he looked at her, as if he might die if he didn't get a taste of her soon.

"You can name your price." She slipped her fingers deeper into his shirt and pulled him closer, so their faces were only inches apart and an urge to kiss him filled her again. His eyes dropped to her lips and they parted, anticipation curling through her as a voice deep in her heart begged him to kiss her instead. "I have plenty of money."

His gaze turned hooded. "What if I don't want money from you?"

She swallowed hard and her courage faltered. "I'm not sure. I'm not the sort to turn tricks for anything."

Not even her life.

She couldn't blame him for putting it out there though. The heat between them was intense, stoked mostly by her and her flirting, and he could probably tell she was close to crawling onto his lap and rubbing herself against him. She frowned at that. What was it about this dark hunter that had her itching for a taste of him and unable to deny the urges running rampant through her?

He was gorgeous, and radiated danger at an intoxicating level, and she always had like men with secrets.

"I wasn't talking about sex," he murmured, loud enough for her sensitive hearing to pick up even with the music pounding through the busy club. His green gaze lifted from her lips to lock with hers. "I was talking about you shifting. I want to see you… I *need* to see you."

Fire blazed through her, heat so intense she couldn't contain it. It scalded her cheeks, sparked by what he had said and the earnest desire in his eyes, a look that backed up his words, instilling them with the need and want he had mentioned.

Cait nodded. "You'll get to see me in my cat form, and I'll pay you… ten grand… if you do this job for me."

He looked satisfied with that offer. "And the job is?"

She opened her mouth and then closed it again when a trickle of fear ran through her, doubts surfacing as she realised what she was asking him to do. She didn't want the male hellcat after her anymore, she wanted him dealt with, but how far was she willing to go to achieve that? The male was strong and determined. What if he hurt Owen? What if he killed him? Could she live with herself knowing that she had gotten the man sitting in front of her killed?

Owen sighed. "I've seen that look before. Believe me… you're not the first to wonder whether I'm up to the task… and believe me… you won't be the first I prove wrong when I'm the last man standing."

The venom in his tone and the determination that flashed in his green eyes told her that he was a man who didn't like having his abilities questioned. She hadn't meant to anger him but she had clearly done just that by pausing to think over what she was asking him to do, and she hadn't even done it because she doubted his abilities.

She had done it because she feared having to watch him die.

She managed a half smile. "I don't doubt you're up to whatever task you set your mind to, Owen… but I'm guessing you've never fought a hellcat before?"

His left eyebrow rose. "Another hellcat?"

She nodded. "A male. Let's just say he thinks like the rest of his kind and believes I ought to just hurl myself at his feet and be his breeding bitch… and I'm of the opinion he can go fuck himself."

His eyebrow dropped and both of them dipped low above eyes that only grew darker when she took a deep breath and tugged the right side of her corset up to reveal the bruise on her ribs. The blow that had caused it had knocked the wind out of her and had pushed her close to shifting from the pain.

"Are they broken?" Owen reached out to touch the bruise but she dropped her top and smoothed it back into place to stop him, afraid of how she might react if he laid his hands on her.

She wasn't sure she would be able to stop herself from touching him back and from there it was only a brief hop to making out with him right here in Underworld and right where everyone could watch. She wouldn't care about the audience either. The passion and need boiling within her were so intense that once she started with Owen, she wouldn't be able to stop until she had burned them out, and probably worn Owen out too.

"No," she said when he lifted green eyes to meet hers again, seeking an answer. "Fractured… but healing."

"When did this happen?" He looked back down at her side, his gaze so intense she felt sure it would burn a hole through her corset.

"Around two hours ago… in an alley near here. I was ambushed… we fought… I escaped."

Owen frowned and lifted his eyes back to her face, a beautiful dark edge to them, one that promised death to whoever had hurt her. "And the male?"

She slid her gaze off to her left, towards the shadowy corner where he still lurked, watching her with Owen.

"Let's just say he's too close to me for my comfort."

Owen looked out of the corner of his eye in the direction she had and the dark slashes of his eyebrows dipped lower. Cait had thought his eyes had held a promise of death before. She had been wrong. The look that had been in them a moment ago was hearts and flowers compared with the one that filled his green eyes now, turning them stormy and deadly.

Cait told herself that she was doing the right thing. Owen Nightingale was infamous. The best hunter there was and a specialist in shifters. If anyone could help her, it was him. He was her best shot at freedom. Her only hope.

She waited for him to look back at her before she poured all of that hope into a question that would pin it all on him.

"Will you take my job?"

CHAPTER 3

Would he take her job?

Owen looked back towards the person she had surreptitiously pointed out, a huge dark-haired man loitering in one of the many corners of the crowded club but not completely swathed in shadows.

His blood began a slow boil at the thought that the man had ambushed Cait just two hours ago, making her have to fight to escape and injuring her in the process. The shifter was exactly the sort of mark he had gone after countless times—a male who thought that females could be subjugated and were put on this planet for their pleasure, created to be at their beck and call.

Little more than a slave.

He narrowed his eyes on the male as the immense shifter looked at him, holding his steady gaze and showing him that he might have Cait running, but he wouldn't get the same reaction out of him.

Owen had put down plenty of his kind.

This male would be just another misogynistic bastard to add to his tally.

He dragged his gaze back to Cait where she sat opposite him, all of her confidence gone, leaving behind a woman who looked smaller and vulnerable to him.

In need of his protection.

He had only just met her, but he didn't like seeing her this way, the light disappeared from her eyes and all of the brightness gone from her face as she waited to hear what he would say.

"I'll take it." Owen offered his hand and she slipped hers into it, her palm soft against his and sending a warm thrill chasing up his arm.

He shook her hand and then released her, leaned down and swiped his black satchel from the floor. Cait's blue eyes followed his every move and widened slightly when he removed his tablet device from his bag and flipped the cover open. He set his bag down on his lap, and the tablet on top of it, and tapped the icon that would start up the database he had created.

The basic program filled the bright screen and he tapped on the search function and selected cat shifters from the list of species. There were so many cat shifter species that he had given them their own category separate from other shifters.

While it loaded all of the shifters he had documented, Owen flagged Sherry down. If he was going to deal with jumping straight into another job, one that might be beyond his skill level, he was going to need another drink.

Sherry bounced along the length of the bar to him, her blonde ponytail swaying with each step.

"Hellfire?" she said with a smile and he grimaced and shook his head.

"Something a little less liable to kill me this time. Two vodkas, on ice. Make it the good stuff."

Sherry nodded and left to make his drinks. The screen on his tablet changed, snagging his attention. He swiped up the screen, scrolling through all the cat shifters he had documented, pausing only long enough to pay Sherry when she returned. She set the drinks down, took his money, and disappeared along the bar.

Owen pushed one of the glasses across to Cait. Her eyes were glued to his tablet, the screen lighting her face as she leaned across, closer to him, her head at an angle.

"These are all shifters you've met?" She ran her gaze over the pictures he had managed to snap of the shifters in secret from a safe distance and hooked her long dark hair behind her ears, pulling it away from her face. "It says two thousand three hundred and twelve results."

He nodded. "That's how many cat shifters I've come across. Not all of them are alive now."

She leaned away from him, a frown marring her brow. "You think he's in there?"

Owen shrugged. "He sounds like the type who might have a rep. I might have come across him before. There's something familiar about him."

He swigged his vodka and altered the parameters of the search to male and height in the six-foot-three to six-foot-six range.

The results came back quicker this time, down to only eight hundred and twenty two.

Cait looked impressed and scanned the page as he scrolled. He was almost at the bottom of the list when she jammed her finger against an entry.

"That's him." Her touch brought the record up and she snatched her hand back and blinked at the screen.

Owen had the impression that she didn't get out of Hell much. "Never seen a tablet before?"

"I have," she said, a hint of indignation in her tone. "I just haven't touched one. I wasn't expecting it to do that."

He smiled as she peered closer to the device, her gaze flitting around the screen.

"You're certain this Marius fellow is him?" Owen waited for her to nod before going back to work.

"Marius," she murmured, still staring at the photograph on the screen. "I think I remember someone shouting that at him once."

He double-tapped the part of the entry where it had the male down as a panther shifter and corrected it. The notes on the sources of information mentioned that eyewitnesses in a Nepal village high in the mountains in snow leopard territory had described him as a black cat. Owen had presumed he was a black panther. He probably hadn't even considered the male could be a hellcat.

"I don't have much on him." But what he did have was enough to ring some warning bells in his head.

The male followed similar patterns to other fae he had tracked, travelling from one prime location for rare species to another. Nepal. Brazil. Northern India. Siberia. All places with rare cat shifters.

Owen studied Cait as she stared at the tablet.

He had a feeling she might be in serious danger but he didn't want to spook her by telling her that the male after her probably dealt in the black market. They were both hellcats. There was an equal chance that Cait was right and Marius wanted her as a mate.

Until he had investigated the male further and had more information on him, Owen would keep his suspicions to himself.

He closed the cover of his tablet device and put it back in his bag.

"I don't go into things blind. I need more information. I think we should go somewhere quieter to discuss the job and so you can fill me in on everything you know… maybe away from your admirer." Owen took his drink and smiled at her, raising the glass at the same time, hoping the male was still watching them.

If luck was with him, Marius wouldn't know who he was and would think he was just another mortal in the bar flirting with Cait. A harmless male looking for a good time.

He instantly hardened in his black jeans, his body issuing a painful reminder that it wasn't wholly a lie. He was looking for a good time with Cait. Her flirting had revved him up, filling his head with thoughts of finding a dark corner and making out with her.

Okay, making out was a little too innocent sounding for what he had in mind, but it had been a while since he had been as attracted to someone as he was to her. Heck, he wasn't sure he had ever been this attracted to anyone. He had always kept his dalliances short and sweet, a periodic scratching of a biological itch, but something about Cait had him firing on all cylinders and thinking in terms longer than a single hot and heavy moment.

He was thinking in terms longer than multiple hot and heavy moments. Nights were involved. Many of them. As many as she would give him.

More than they might have together when working on her job.

He emptied his glass to kill that thought with the alcohol and set it back down on the bar.

"Where do you want to go?" She sipped her drink, a genuine smile playing on her lips and the fire back in her eyes. It sent a bolt of hot lust through him again and he grimaced and shifted on his seat, trying to get more comfortable as his jeans pinched his groin.

"My place." It came out a little harder and more demanding, and definitely more hungry than he had intended.

Her eyes widened a fraction before narrowing on his and filling with dark desire that left him in no doubt she was thinking wicked things too, her mind leaping forwards to picture what awaited her at his place.

Owen ground his teeth and shot for professional. "We can discuss the job further there and you'll be safe, off the radar of your male."

"He's not my male." She leaned towards him and he leaned back, cursing himself when her smile faded and her gaze lost its heat and hunger. She bounced back, taking another swig of her drink and smiling again. "We can go to your place. I'm intrigued. I want to know what a hunter's home looks like."

Owen grimaced for a different reason as he pictured it in his head and realised he was about to make a heck of a poor impression.

He took a small silver glass vial from his bag, tipped half of the contents into his empty glass, and knocked it back. The alcohol haze instantly evaporated, leaving his head clear. He always had loved this particular elixir. Tipsy to sober in a heartbeat. A weapon that should be in any good hunter's arsenal and one that had saved his life a few times. There were plenty of demons and fae out there who saw a drunk hunter and figured it was a good time to take them out of action. His little elixir solved that problem for him. One swift chug and he was fighting fit and it was the opportunistic non-human who was taken out of action by him.

He turned and looked over his left shoulder, along the bar, searching for Kyter. The sandy-haired shifter was nowhere to be seen but the big silver-haired male who worked behind the bar with Kyter noticed him and strolled towards him.

When the man reached him, Owen said, "Can we slip out the back?"

The bartender looked between him and Cait, a dark edge to his eyes as he folded his arms across his chest, causing the sleeves of his white shirt to stretch tight across his muscles. Owen had the feeling he was going to say no.

He turned to face the big shifter. "There's a male harassing her."

The bartender's stormy eyes shifted back to her and lingered for a moment before he jerked his chin towards the opposite end of the bar and walked away.

Owen slipped from his stool, took hold of Cait's wrist, and led her through the throng around the bar, using it as cover. He kept low and she did the same, skulking through the crowd behind him. Her other hand caught hold of his wrist as someone jostled her and he pulled her closer, looking back to check on her at the same time, fearing for a moment the male had come after her.

It was just the normal crush around the bar and the human man who had bumped her muttered an apology.

Owen stopped at the end of the bar and peered to his left through a gap in the people there, making sure that the huge male lurking in the shadows was looking in the wrong direction before he made a break for the dark door just beyond the bar where the silver-haired male waited for them.

The man opened the dark metal door in the black back wall of the club as they swiftly approached and closed it as soon as they were through.

The brightly lit cavernous pale room was a contrast to the loud dark main room of the club, quiet enough that Owen could hear his ears ringing from the assault of the music and could hear Cait breathing. She turned on the spot, taking everything in, from the doors that led off the large space to his right to the staircase against the left wall that led upwards. He headed straight for the exit near the foot of the stairs that would take them out into a narrow alley behind the club. His car was parked nearby.

Owen adjusted the strap of his bag on his shoulder and took hold of Cait's arm again as he headed for the back door. It wasn't the first time he'd had to exit the club this way, but normally it was because someone had decided to try to claim the glory of killing him. This was the first time he had left because of a job. It was also the first time he had left the club with a woman.

A woman he was intending to take back to his place.

Another first for him.

His father's string of marriages after the death of Owen's mother had led to Owen keeping a firm grip on his heart, never allowing anything to happen that might compromise it. Right at the top of the list of risks he wasn't willing to take was bringing a woman back to his place. He looked back over his shoulder at Cait as he opened the emergency exit door.

She smiled at him, one that reached her blue eyes and set them alight again, restoring the confident woman who had caught his eye and had him enraptured.

Bringing her back to his home felt like a dangerous move. One liable to weaken the barriers he had constructed to stop himself from falling foul of the same pitfalls as his father.

It was on the tip of his tongue to say he had changed his mind and they should go somewhere else when she shifted closer to him, her other hand coming up in a protective gesture to hover over her chest. Her eyes darted both ways along the dark alley and he swore he felt her trembling beneath his fingers.

His need to take care of her roared back to the fore, vanquishing his fears, and he tugged her along the alley towards the quiet road at the end of it. He didn't release her until he had dug his keys out of his bag, unlocked his small black hatchback, and had the door open for her. She thanked him with another electric smile that sent a thousand volts sparking along his nerve endings, setting them alight, and slipped into the passenger seat.

Owen closed the door, rounded the compact car and slid into the driver's seat. He twisted at the waist and put his bag on the back seat, and then put the key into the ignition and started the car. The engine growled to life and he flicked the switch for the lights, checked the road and pulled out. He tugged his seatbelt on as he drove and glanced across at Cait.

"Buckle up." He waited to see she was doing as instructed, tugging the slim black belt across her chest, before returning his focus to the road.

It was quiet, the night drawing on, making it easy going as he navigated the short journey deep into an affluent neighbourhood near the centre of London.

Cait's eyes grew wider by the moment as she stared out of the windows, taking in the buildings. When he drove through large black wrought iron gates, her eyes shot impossibly wide and she looked across at him. He kept his eyes on the road, unwilling to field her silent question, slowing the car as he drove through the rows of beautiful pale townhouses.

He turned left down another side road where the biggest houses were located and pulled the car into a reserved parking spot outside his one. Cait was still staring at him. He turned the engine off, undid his seatbelt, gathered his bag, and stepped out of the car.

She followed him a moment later, her eyebrows pinned high on her forehead as she finally looked away from him, her gaze settling on the huge four storey Georgian townhouse behind him.

"What you pictured?" he said before locking the car and turning his back on her. He strode towards the short black iron gate, opened it and glanced over his shoulder at her.

She hurried towards him, her eyes flitting between him and the house.

It was too big for him.

He used the sum total of five rooms out of the possible fourteen.

"This is yours?" She spoke at last, her gaze on the white townhouse, slowly drifting up the height of it.

Owen walked up the path, took the steps up to the covered porch with its Grecian columns, and unlocked the wide black wooden door. He pushed it open, proving it was his.

"It belongs to my family," he said as way of an explanation when she looked at him again. "It costs a small fortune to run, but I haven't been able to bring myself to part with it."

"You grew up here." It wasn't a question. She looked him right in the eye as she said it, her expression sober, and he nodded.

It wasn't often he met someone who could see straight through him as Cait could. Most people didn't seem to understand him at all.

The humans he met who weren't hunters, and therefore were unaware of the world of fae and demons that co-existed with theirs, weren't worth his time. He had nothing he could talk about with them, not as normal people did. He couldn't gripe about his work week over a beer with a buddy. The hunters avoided him because he wasn't aligned with any of the organisations they worked for and only exchanged information when it suited them.

The fae and demons preferred to keep him at arm's length because of his profession.

The only people he could really talk to and who had ever understood him were his family, and those who had been closest to him were dead now. He had a handful of relatives remaining, mostly from his mother's side, and he rarely saw them.

"You live here alone." Cait's soft voice drew him out of his thoughts and he sighed as he looked at her where she now stood on the porch beside him, close enough that he could smell her sweet perfume on the night breeze.

He nodded again. "I keep most of the rooms closed and use just the ones I need... bathroom, bedroom... living room... kitchen. I did make one of the other reception rooms into a gym and training room."

She looked as if she was on the verge of saying it sounded lonely, so he turned his back on her, stepped into the hall and switched on the lights. Thankfully, she took the hint and remained silent as she entered behind him and closed the door.

Owen locked it and pocketed his keys. "Come on. I'll get you settled in the living room."

He led the way up the wooden staircase to the first floor and the large pale blue room he used for his living room. He grimaced as he realised he had left it in a worse state than he had thought.

Cait drifted past him before he could say anything in warning, a twinkle in her eyes as they danced over all of the weapons spread across the large oak table on the left side of the room, and all the knickknacks he had left strewn across the square wooden coffee table nestled in the U of his three black leather couches in front of the fireplace.

She ambled around the room and he watched her as she allowed her fingers to drift over a few items on the coffee table and checked out some of his weapons.

"It looks very much as I had expected in here." She lifted her eyes away from the crossbow she held and smiled across the room at him. "I imagined weapons and books."

She looked around at the stacked bookcases that lined the wall to his right between the tall sash windows and the one behind him, and then down at the sheets of paper, notepads, and newspapers stacked haphazardly on a smaller coffee table beside an armchair.

"Although... it has an air of bachelor about it too." Her smile teased him and he shrugged.

She hadn't seen his bedroom.

If she thought this room looked like a bachelor owned it, she was in for a shock if she set eyes on his inner sanctum.

Her blue eyes drifted over the couches and then roamed back to him, gaining a dark edge of desire that set his pulse pounding and left him feeling she might just want to see that inner sanctum.

He was damned if she was going to see it as it was though.

He wasn't sure how hellcats lived, or what accommodation they were used to, but he was fairly certain that as a woman she wasn't impressed by clothes strewn across the floor, unmade beds, and several empty take out cartons, and that was exactly what his bedroom contained.

"You seem to favour magic." Cait set the crossbow down and Owen stared at her, his heart pounding for a different reason as he took in what she had said. When she frowned and gestured to all the knickknacks covering the coffee table, his gaze leaped there and his heart settled. "The items... they're magic aren't they?"

Owen quickly nodded. "I get them in the fae town nearby. Some I use, others are just part of a collection."

He backed towards the door.

"You like magic?" She looked at him again.

Owen took another step backwards and gave a noncommittal shrug in answer.

"I have to get changed and get some stuff together. Make yourself comfortable."

He turned and walked out of the room, feeling her gaze boring into his back, intense and focused, as if she was trying to strip away the layers of his defences to uncover a truth he preferred to keep hidden.

A secret he'd had for most of his life and had kept from his father.

A secret only one living person in this world knew.

CHAPTER 4

Cait could only blink as Owen made a swift exit, leaving her standing in the centre of the eggshell blue room. She looked around, wondering what he expected her to do while he changed, and why he had felt the sudden need to do such a thing. Sometimes, on rare occasions, she didn't understand males.

She sighed, sat on the leather couch opposite the black marble fireplace and perused the magical items on the square wooden table again. There were many different types. Some looked as if they were meant for defence, while others appeared to be used to heal.

Her gaze drifted to a not so magical healing item near the right corner of the table. A white bottle of pills. She carefully turned the pot around and read the label. Prescription medicine of some kind. She wasn't familiar with the name of the contents.

She placed her palms on her knees and sat in silence for a while, staring at the unlit fire, listening for a sign of Owen. She wasn't sure how many minutes had passed since he had rushed from the room, but she felt certain he wasn't going to return anytime soon.

Cait slid her gaze towards the weapons and then to the door behind her. She was sure he wouldn't mind if she looked around a little. It could be considered making herself comfortable.

She rose to her feet and padded around the room, snooping at his books first. Most of them were tomes about different species, but others were diaries. She read several interesting entries dated from before she had been born over four centuries ago, and then set the book back on the wooden shelf. She trailed the fingers of her right hand across the spines of the others as she walked, heading towards the wall with the fireplace.

Several portraits hung on the wall, all of them old, and all of them resembling Owen in some way. His family. The men in the paintings had regal bearings, an air of importance about them. That contrasted against Owen. He didn't seem to share their sense of conceited pride.

He had pride, definitely, but not the sort these men in their portraits possessed, a sense of entitlement and that they were better than others, elevated by their cause.

Cait wandered on, bored with staring at his ancestors when she wanted to see him, and snuck towards the door. She peered out of it and into the long hallway. The dark green paint and rich wooden floor seemed to suck the light out of the space, turning the mounted and stuffed heads on the walls even more sinister.

She hoped he didn't intend to add a hellcat head to the array of Hell beasts he had on display. She couldn't imagine what visitors made of the gigantic, scaly or horned beast heads.

Cait glanced back into the living room and mulled over the way Owen had acted since they had arrived at his home.

He probably didn't have many visitors.

She was beginning to doubt he had any and that she was the first person other than Owen to set foot in this house in a very long time.

She turned back towards the hallway and froze as her gaze fell on one of the huge mounted heads.

A shiver ran down her spine and she bared her small fangs at the beast that appeared as a blend between a lion and a reptile, hating the way the red eyes seemed to follow her. She had come close to losing her life to one of those wretched monsters more than once while in Hell. They hunted in packs, rabid beasts that didn't stop once they caught the scent of fresh meat. The only way to get them off your tail was killing them.

Or craftily crossing paths with an unsuspecting demon and using him as a decoy that would then become the target of the pack's hunt.

Cait had no regrets about using such tactics. Demons could teleport. She couldn't. They were far more likely to survive a pack of Hell beasts than she was and if they didn't, it was one less demon in the world. As a creature born of the Devil's domain, it could be considered her civic duty to dispose of as many of the demons who had revolted against him and set up their own realms in Hell.

A bang echoed through the house.

She snarled and leaped back into the living room, breathing hard as adrenaline surged through her veins and her senses stretched out, seeking what had caused the sudden noise.

Nothing.

She huffed and smoothed her long black hair, trying to calm herself with the motion. It wasn't like her to be so jittery but the fight with the male hellcat had set her on edge. She had spent most of the night on high alert, constantly aware of the male on a subconscious level, fearing he would attack her again. Even after she had left with Owen through the back door, she hadn't been able to settle down. She had spent the entire journey wriggling in her seat and using the side mirrors to look behind her, convinced the male was following her somehow.

What if he had?

An ominous whining sound ran through the building, followed by banging and rattling.

Cait forced herself to stay where she was and ignore it. It was nothing. Probably just the house.

What if it *was* something?

What if it was *him*?

Her heart exploded into action and she rushed to the large oak table filled with weapons and armed herself with a crossbow. Her hands shook as she loaded it, drawing the string back into position and settling the dart into its cradle. She raised it and looked around the room, pointing the weapon wherever her gaze fell, breathing hard and fighting her ridiculous fear.

The banging came again, louder this time.

Cait raced from the room, tracking Owen's scent through the building, following it down the green corridor and up another staircase. A softer noise came from ahead of her together with movement on her senses and she bolted in that direction, throwing a panicked glance over her shoulder at the same time, convinced someone was closing in on her in the dark hallway.

A strip of light shone from beneath a wooden door at the end of the corridor.

She shouldered that door open. "I heard something."

She swung her gaze towards Owen and stopped dead.

The sudden jerk to a halt made her finger depress the trigger on the crossbow and the bolt zipped across the room, shot just above Owen's left shoulder and thudded into the cream wall behind him where he stood right in front of her.

Naked.

Both of his hands moved in unison, racing to cover himself.

Water dripped from the tangled threads of his dark brown hair, rolled down his sculpted cheekbones and the strong line of his square jaw, and dropped from there to cascade in enticing rivulets down the defined muscles of his chest. Those glistening trails lured her eyes downwards, over the ridges of his abdomen and past the sensual dip of his navel to the dusting of dark hair that captured her gaze and had her face heating as desire flared hotter in her veins.

Cait stared at his hands for long seconds, entranced and dumbstruck, unable to gather her wits or acknowledge the voice in her head that was screaming at her to look away and give him some privacy because she was probably making him uncomfortable.

His fingers flexed where he cupped himself, weakening the spell the sight of him had cast on her, enough that she managed to drag her eyes up to his.

A touch of colour darkened his cheeks.

"I heard something," Cait muttered, falling deeper under his spell again as her eyes betrayed her and dropped back to his body.

Rope after delicious rope of honed powerful muscles delighted her eyes as she focused on his body rather than the tracks of water and she couldn't stop herself from gawping at him, drinking in the incredible sight of him naked, even when she tried with all of her will to look away again.

Owen cleared his throat but his voice still came out a little squeaky. "It's the water pipes. I should have warned you. I took a shower."

Cait nodded dumbly. She could see that, and she couldn't help imagining it too. She swallowed hard, heating to a thousand degrees as she stared at him, picturing him standing under a spray of water, rivulets of it coursing down over his muscles in a constant stream.

She shook herself and finally managed to gain enough control to turn away, giving him the privacy he deserved.

"Sorry." She scratched the back of her neck with one hand and lowered the crossbow she held in the other.

The weight of it brought back her awareness of the weapon.

Gods, she had almost shot him too.

She wasn't sure what she would have done if she had actually hit him. She cringed. It certainly would have made a terrible impression on him. It was bad enough that she had come sprinting into his room like a scared child, frightened by the sounds of water pipes groaning. She shook her head, despairing as she realised that he probably had a dire opinion of her already and it was completely wrong.

Normally, she was confident and able, a skilled fighter and an independent woman who could stand on her own two feet and didn't need a male to take care of her. She had survived four centuries of life, most of that in Hell, and had been the victor in too many battles to count and outwitted her opponents in the rest.

Today was not a normal day though.

The ambush had thrown her off kilter and then Owen had knocked her even more off balance.

She set the crossbow down on the dark blue covers of the double bed in front of her and stared at it, slowly gathering her strength and pulling herself back together.

Owen moved around the room behind her.

Cait closed her eyes, because she knew that if she didn't, she would end up trying to catch another glimpse of him as he dried off and dressed.

Not that he gave her a chance to steal a peek.

"Done," he said and she opened her eyes and turned to face him, surprised at how quickly he had dressed.

Or hadn't dressed.

He stood before her wearing only a pair of black jeans that rode low on his hips, rubbing a small pale towel across his short hair.

Cait noticed something other than how honed and godly his body was as she looked at him this time.

She noticed all the dark bruises and the cuts that littered his arms, shoulders, sides and even parts of his stomach. He turned away from her, revealing a particularly nasty bruise on his left side, just above his bottom. She drifted towards him, staring at it and reaching out to touch it.

Owen spun to face her.

Cait jumped and snatched her hand back, her eyes leaping up to meet his pale green ones.

"Where did you get all the bruises?" she said, trying to make it clear she'd had a reason for wanting to touch him, one other than the desire pulsing through her again, steadily building back up towards a crescendo.

"The demon a few fae hired me to kill didn't take kindly to my opinion that he should die for terrorising them. We had a little bit of an argument about it a couple of days ago." Owen looked himself over and prodded a small mottled bruise on the ridge of muscle that curved over his right hip. "They'll be gone in a few days. I just have to keep applying my salve to them."

She was about to ask what he meant by that when he leaned across to his right, picked up a small black glass pot from the wooden dressing table beside him and opened it.

Cait flinched away as the smell hit her.

Aniseed.

She pulled a face at it. She never had liked that smell.

"It doesn't stink as bad once it's on," Owen said, his deep voice curling around her, making her forget the offensive smell of his salve for a moment.

She looked up at him to find him staring at the pot, a flicker of something in his green eyes. When they leaped back to her, darkening a degree, revealing his desire again, she realised why he was concerned about the smell, and her reaction to it.

The heat inside her exploded into an inferno again, burning up her blood as she stared into his eyes, filled with a need to take him up on his silent offer.

She wanted her taste of him now.

Gods, she hoped he was right and the salve did smell less disgusting when it was on.

She wanted to tell him to forget it, at least for a while. She could apply it later, massaging it into his bruises and wounds while he lay on the bed, spent from their lovemaking.

He looked as if he was considering such a thing himself but then sighed wearily and stuck his right index finger into the gunk.

He smoothed a little of it over each of his cuts and his bruises, and she couldn't help but smile when she noticed he was doing his best not to grimace as he rubbed it in. Trying to look strong and manly in her presence? It reassured her a little. After all, she had been worried about appearing like a weak kitten in need of coddling too.

Owen twisted at the waist and grimaced, sucking in a sharp breath through his teeth.

"I can do your back." The words were out of her lips before she could consider what she was offering.

It wasn't the smell of the salve that had her regretting her offer as he nodded, because it smelled oddly sweet now that it was on him, as if the properties of it had changed somehow.

It was the fact that she was about to touch him, running her fingers over his bare flesh while standing in the middle of his bedroom.

Owen held the black glass pot out to her and Cait took it, stared at it and drew in a deep breath to steady herself as he turned his back to her. There were more bruises on his back, long deep ones that looked as if the demon had thrown him into something unbreakable. In amidst the bruises were slashes, easily recognisable as claw marks. They were scabbed over and healing, but they must have been deep when they had happened.

She looked down at the creamy salve, wondering what magic was in the concoction, because nothing made by human hands could heal such terrible wounds in such a short space of time.

How many times had he relied on this same potion to heal his wounds for him? How many times had he been beaten this badly, or worse, by his enemies?

How badly injured would he end up when he took care of Marius for her?

She gripped the pot and stared at it, her stomach turning to lead and dragging her insides down to her feet. She shook her head. She couldn't ask Owen to handle the male for her. Owen was strong, but the hellcat was stronger. She knew from first-hand experience just how strong that male was.

What had she been thinking?

"Cait?" The sound of her name rolling off Owen's tongue in his deep steady voice soothed her.

Owen wasn't facing Marius alone. She would be there with him and she had to have faith in him, as she had back in the bar, before her attraction to him had begun to place doubts in her head and fear in her heart.

"Sorry," she muttered again and stuck her fingers into the pot.

The salve was cold, strangely so, and the smell changed from aniseed when it was on her fingers to a sweet sugary smell when she rubbed it into the first bruise on his back, a deep one that covered half of his left shoulder-blade.

"I don't always end up looking like a Friesian cow." There was a warm note in Owen's voice that suggested he was making a joke but she didn't get it.

She smoothed more of the salve into the bruise, keeping her strokes light so she didn't hurt him. "A cow?"

"A Friesian cow." He looked back over his shoulder at her, his green eyes bright with his stunning smile. The light in them faded as he frowned. "You have no clue what I'm talking about, do you?"

She shook her head.

He sighed and turned away from her again. "It's a black and white cow... like a white cow with black splotches on it... you do know what a cow is?"

Cait chuckled. "Of course. I've seen cows. I didn't realise they had special names. You're referencing this cow in relation to your black marks against your paler skin."

He heaved another sigh. "When you say it like that, it doesn't sound funny."

Cait dipped her fingers back into the pot, scooped a small quantity of the creamy gunk up, and applied it to a series of smaller bruises and cuts that dotted his right shoulder.

"I didn't mean to make it not funny... I'm not sure this is really something you should laugh about either." Her work slowed as she again thought about how a demon had done this much damage to him.

The male hellcat had hurt her and he was stronger than a measly demon. What would he do to Owen?

"If you keep doubting me... we're going to fall out." Those words leaving Owen's lips in a cold dead voice sent a chill through her.

How did he know whenever she was doubting him? Did he have abilities that were beyond human? Could he sense things as fae and demons could? She had the feeling it had been more than what she had said that had alerted him to her thoughts about him losing to the male.

Owen looked back over his shoulder at her again, his green eyes as dark as they had been when he had eyed Marius. Another shiver went through her when they met hers, holding her immobile.

"I can handle your male." The certainty in those five words and in his eyes gave her some relief, but riled her at the same time.

"He isn't my male." She looked away from him. "I don't have a male."

"Don't have and don't want?"

Cait let his words hang in the air between them as she dealt with another of his bruises, focusing on it to avoid his questioning gaze.

Her movements slowed as he continued to stare at her, her fingers drifting across his skin and awareness of how close they were to each other rising inside her. Heat rose with it, bringing her desire and need back to inferno level, until each tiny stroke of her fingers over his flesh had arcs of electric tingles rushing over her skin.

Her breathing quickened, the air too thick and heavy, making her head spin as she struggled to focus on her task and not how good he felt beneath her questing fingers.

She swept those fingers over the bruise on his left side, feeling his heat radiating from him and through her.

"Cait." His deep voice scraped low, a husky whisper that sent a thrill coursing through her and brought all of her focus upwards as he slowly turned to face her.

She lifted her eyes to his, her fingers resting against his side, desire pulsing through her.

Passion that flared white-hot as she waited to see what he would do.

He wanted her. She knew that. She had felt it back at the club and she felt it clearer now, a deep primal awareness that he desired her. Fiercely needed her.

She wanted him too.

Something about him was irresistible.

It had drawn her to him from the moment she had set eyes on him and she had been burning for him ever since, on fire with a need to feel his arms around her and his lips claiming hers.

His green eyes darkened, narrowing hungrily on hers.

Cait breathed harder, anticipation swirling through her and stealing the air from her lungs as she willed him to surrender to his need, to give in to the passion beating in his veins and drumming in his heart because she felt it too. It consumed her. Controlled her.

And she couldn't deny it any longer.

The pot fell from her fingers and smashed on the wooden floor.

CHAPTER 5

The second the glass pot shattered on the wooden floor, Owen swept Cait up into his arms and claimed her mouth, unable to hold back any longer. He groaned in time with her as his lips clashed with hers, the kiss frantic and wild, an outpouring of the desire that had been constantly building in him all night, never truly abating.

During talking business with her, during the drive to his home, and even during the time they had been apart while he had taken a very cold shower, it had been growing stronger, consuming and devouring him, demanding he throw aside all conventions and take her as he wanted to.

He grabbed her backside, easily lifted her feet off the floor and walked to the bed with her as he kissed her harder. She responded sweetly, her hands clutching his bare shoulders and her lips attempting to dominate his, stealing control of the kiss. The pleasure coursing through him was so intense that he didn't feel the pain of his bruises as she held on to him, her fingertips pressing into his flesh.

He didn't give her control either.

His little kitty had fire, but she wouldn't get her way, not this time.

He was too hungry for her, burning too hot, beyond all control.

Owen dropped her on the blue covers of his double bed and instantly covered her with his body, wedging his hips between her thighs.

She moaned and dug her right hand into his dark hair, twisting the longer lengths around her fingers and grasping them. He mirrored her, clutching the nape of her neck as he kissed her, his fingers palming her flesh as he held her tightly, pinning her mouth to his and not letting her escape. She was his in this moment and she would know it.

He angled his head and deepened the kiss, thrusting his tongue past her lips as he rocked his hips between her thighs. Her sweet moan tore a groan from his throat and he thrust harder, his moan becoming a grunt of frustration when his jeans and her tight black leather trousers hindered him.

Owen shoved onto his knees. They slipped off the end of the bed and he landed on his feet, not breaking his stride as he went for her leathers. He popped the button and slid the zip down, his entire body quaking as his gaze hungrily followed his hands. Cait wriggled backwards on the bed and grabbed her trousers beside her hips. She shimmied out of them, shoving them down her slender thighs, revealing toned perfectly pale skin for his eyes to devour.

He groaned and helped her, removing her boots and tossing them behind him. Each one landed with a thud that drew a smile from Cait that grew wider as she finally wrestled free of her tight trousers. She kicked them away from her and Owen grabbed her ankles. He slid his hands over her calves as he kneeled on the bed, looking down into her eyes, transfixed by how blue they were around her dilated pupils. Like ice-cold fire.

She was anything but cold though.

She was burning up beneath his palms as he stroked his way up her legs, holding them in the air, one on either side of his hips.

He stared down at her, loving how her breathing accelerated, her breasts pressing against the top of her dark corset, threatening to spill out. He licked his lips and her gaze darkened, her eyes dropping to his mouth and then drifting lower, over his bare chest. Heat travelled in the wake of her hungry eyes as they raked over him and he couldn't control himself when the soft pink tip of her tongue swept over her lower lip.

He dropped onto all fours over her and kissed her again, seizing those lips and tasting her heat and her passion.

"Owen," she murmured against his lips and wrapped her legs around him, dragging him down against her.

A flicker of awareness pierced the haze of lust in his mind and he pushed himself up, removing his weight from her.

She glared at him and tried to pull him back down.

"Your ribs." He held firm, his gaze falling to the right side of her corset.

"Almost healed," she whispered breathlessly. "If you think we're stopping because of them, you're thinking with the wrong head and I know just the way to get you back on track."

She wedged her hand between their bodies and rubbed his aching shaft through his jeans, ripping a moan from him as his eyes rolled closed, his arms trembled under his weight and his hips shifted of their own accord, driving him against her palm. Fuck, but she was right. If she wasn't going to raise his injuries as obstacles to what was about to happen between them, he had no right to bring up hers. The pain was nothing to him right now. All that mattered was the pleasure.

Her legs tightened around him as she drew her hand away from him and he gave in to her, pressing his body into hers so he could continue to reap a glimmer of pleasure from driving against her.

She moaned as he rocked between her thighs, grinding his hard length into her sweet spot. Heck, he needed to be naked again. It wasn't enough. He shouldn't have put the damned jeans on. He should have crossed the room to her when she had come running into it, grabbed her and kissed her.

It seemed he wasn't the only one frustrated by a lack of skin contact.

Cait shoved him up off her and growled, the feral snarl echoing around the room and sending a shiver sprinting down his spine as she tore at his jeans, yanking the button fly open. He opened his mouth to comment on her wickedness but she wrapped her hot little hand around his length and words failed him. All he could manage was a garbled groan as bliss skated through him, hot and drugging.

His eyes slipped shut and his arms shook as he braced himself above her, enduring the sensual glide of her hand up and down his cock. She drifted her thumb over the crown and he shuddered, another moan escaping his lips. Her gaze bore into him and he struggled to open his eyes, wanting to see the desire in hers, the passion and need. He would fulfil all of them for her.

He rocked once into her palm, giving himself the brief flicker of pure pleasure, and then pulled himself together.

He stroked the fingers on his right hand across the flat plane of her stomach below her corset and then lower, teasing the elastic of her black lace knickers. She arched upwards, her fingers tightening their hold on his shaft, her desire pulsing through him. He did as she wanted, angling his hand and slipping his fingers beneath the material, seeking her moist centre. She tipped her head back and groaned as he slid his fingers between her plush petals and teased her nub with soft swirls and flicks.

"Owen."

Heck, he could get used to the sound of her purring his name like that, as if only he could give her the pleasure and release, the bliss that she craved.

He swooped on her lips again and she fought back, kissing him hard, each sweep of her lips across his growing in desperation as he teased her towards climax. She began to rock, thrusting her hips upwards, rubbing herself against his fingers. Owen couldn't take it. He couldn't stop himself from imagining being between her thighs as she did that, riding each thrust of his body into hers.

He grunted and snatched his hand out of her knickers, and a flicker of disappointment crossed her face before her eyes darkened again when he tugged her underwear. Her hand slipped from his cock and she helped him, shoving her knickers down her thighs and lifting her legs into the air.

Owen forgot what he was meant to be doing and stared at the sight of her with her legs together in the air, presenting her bottom and soft dark curls to him.

His heart drummed against his chest and his shaft kicked against his stomach, throbbing with need.

He pushed his black jeans down his thighs and caught Cait's ankles as she went to lower her legs. He placed one ankle on each of his shoulders and her gaze darkened further, overflowing with arousal that called to him, telling him to surrender to his own needs as she was surrendering to hers.

Owen slid his hand down her thighs to her backside and raised it off the bed. Her legs drifted down his arms as he leaned over her, catching on his elbows, and her hot gaze slid down the length of his torso, settling on his cock. It jerked again and she murmured the sexiest little moan he had ever heard.

He groaned, grasped his length and stared down at it as he lowered his hips and rubbed the head down her moist flesh. She moaned again as he nudged inside and he groaned along with her as he grasped her backside with both hands and eased his cock into her sheath. The position allowed him to slide as deep as she could take him, every inch of him filling and stretching her. He lingered a moment, absorbing how hot and wet she was, ready for him.

Hungry for him.

Cait's gaze turned hooded as she tilted her head back and rotated her hips, ripping a grunt from his lips. His restraint shattered and he leaned over her, curling her beneath him with her backside in the air, and pressed his hands into the mattress as he thrust into her, long deep strokes that matched the fierce rhythm of his heart.

She threw her arms above her head and clutched the pillows as he drove into her, each powerful thrust threatening to jerk her breasts from her corset as they bounced in time with his movements. Her blue eyes brightened, the flicker of fire growing stronger in them, until they glowed from beneath her long black lashes and he couldn't stop staring into them as he moved inside her.

She stole his breath away.

She twisted her hands in the blue covers, dragging them down, her mewls ringing in his ears, each cry making him burn hotter for her. He needed more of her. He needed all of her at once.

He grabbed her hip in his left hand and let her leg slip off his right arm. He leaned over her, burning with a need to kiss her again. She craned her neck and released the covers to reach for him. Her black nails pressed into his shoulders and the nape of his neck, and she dragged him down to her, her lips clashing with his as he thrust into her.

Her sweet moan of bliss was ambrosia on his tongue and he released her hip, allowing her other leg to fall, and then clutched it again, raising her backside off the mattress once more. He leaned on his right elbow, placing his arm beneath her, and curled his fingers over her shoulder, gripping it hard as he moved inside her, each meeting of their bodies tearing another addictive moan from her lips.

Her fingers tensed against him, short claws pressing into his skin. He didn't care if she scratched him. She could go wild. She could let go. He wouldn't care, as long as this didn't end. It felt too good as she began rocking against him, writhing on his cock with each press and slide into her.

"Owen," she moaned and the world sped past him in a blur as she rolled with him, ending up astride him.

Her hands came down hard on his bare chest, pinning him to the bed, and she threw her head back as she rode him, a look of sheer bliss on her pretty face as her red lips parted on a sigh of pleasure. Her eyes locked with his, hooded and dark with desire, the obsidian make-up that surrounded them making them appear impossibly blue now. They entranced him all over again and he fell into them, losing himself in the moment with her.

She lowered her face towards him and the long tangled threads of her black hair fell down over her breasts and obscured them. Each glide of her body on his caused her hair to sway, revealing the tempting dusky peaks of her nipples where they showed above the line of her corset. He wanted to sit up, wrap his arms around her and suckle those nipples until she screamed his name in pleasure, but her hands held him immobile, a willing slave to her.

Owen grabbed her hips and moved with her, thrusting up each time she came down, breathing hard as he struggled to hold back the release he could feel coming.

His balls tightened, drawing up, and his cock thickened, growing harder as release boiled at its base. He grunted and she dug her claws into his chest, her face screwing up as she moaned breathlessly. Spots of red bloomed where her black nails pressed into his chest, the pain nothing but a mild buzz in the back of his mind, drowned out by the roar of pleasure that tore through him as she cried out and convulsed forwards, her body throbbing around his.

He managed three more thrusts before he joined her, his length pulsing as he pinned her down on it and shot his seed deep into her. He moaned with each throb, every hot shiver of bliss that tripped through him in response as he laid claim to her body. Cait moaned with him, her hips quivering beneath his hands, shaking worse than he was.

She smiled lazily and then drifted down to rest on his chest, her heart thundering against his as she breathed hard.

She was soft and hot against him, her body still entwined with his, and he couldn't resist running his hands up and down her spine and corset as he slowly pieced himself back together.

35

Cait drew in a deeper breath and stiffened and he thought he had done something wrong until she spoke.

"I cut you." She pushed herself up, a flicker of concern in her blue eyes as they darted over the marks on his chest.

"I don't mind," he husked and kept rubbing her back, savouring how good she felt beneath his hands and on top of him. "I'm made of sterner stuff than you think. I can handle a few cuts and bruises... especially if they're coming from you and like this."

A touch of rose coloured her cheeks and she averted her gaze, pinning it on the crumpled covers to his left.

Owen lifted his right hand and brushed his fingers across her cheek, studying her as she stared at the bed.

"Cait," he murmured and she eventually looked back at him, down into his eyes, hers filled with a mixture of warmth and something that looked like concern but seemed to run deeper than that emotion. He sighed and brushed her long black hair behind her ear. "You don't have to fear... I won't let him near you... and I won't lose to him. I've fought stronger foes and survived."

"I know. I do believe in you, Owen. I know all the tales. Your name is legendary in Hell."

He might have smiled at that and his heart might have swelled with pride had she not looked so serious and sober.

"Then what is it?" He smoothed his fingers across her cheek and tried to search her eyes but she withdrew from him, closing them and shutting him out.

Owen drew her down to him, settling her back against his chest, and forced himself to let it go, because part of him knew why she feared.

He knew because he feared it too.

He feared she would leave when the job was done and she was free to live her life again.

He feared she would be the first woman to truly break his heart.

Because he feared he was going to make the ultimate mistake.

He was going to fall in love for the first time in his life.

CHAPTER 6

Cait followed Owen down the steps carved into the stone at one end of the enormous cavern that contained a whole fae town. It stretched before her, a mixture of styles of buildings and sizes. Directly below her to her right was the witches' district, denoted by a huge arched sign at the entrance to the widest thoroughfare. The buildings there were mostly square, single-storey and white-washed, with a few rare buildings dotted around the tightly packed cluster that had two storeys, and one even had three.

Colourful canopies reached outwards from the stores, stretching across the network of narrow cobbled streets and almost touching the one belonging to the opposite building. Some of the jewel-toned canopies had crests on them or the name of the shop written in the fae tongue.

Beneath the canopies were huge terracotta urns, stacks of smaller pots, and some baskets and copper stills. The whole area smelled of magic to her, a rich and spicy quality to the air that drifted up to her as she walked down behind Owen.

He adjusted his small black satchel on his shoulder and rolled up the sleeves of his black shirt, his green gaze fixed ahead of him, not once straying to the town below them. Didn't he find it interesting? It fascinated her.

Witches weren't the only species who made it their home and peddled their wares here, running businesses and making a living. There was a district for demons too, in the opposite corner of the cavern behind her. The buildings there were made of black wooden beams and white panels, and had crooked dark tiled roofs.

At the far end, off to her right and beyond the witches' and demons' districts there were numerous larger buildings constructed against the side of the cavern.

When they reached the bottom of the steps, Owen caught hold of her wrist and guided her through the crowd, falling in with the flow of foot traffic around the town. She had to fight to remain close to him as they tried to cut across the people swiftly moving to and from the witches' district.

Cait wasn't surprised by the popularity of the stores there. Witches peddled everything from poisons to love potions. Whatever you needed, they could supply.

She had half a mind to pick up a poison she could use on the male after her, or maybe something to reignite the lust in Owen's veins, but he didn't give her a chance to take a peek at the stores. He dragged her down a series of alleyways between the buildings that were sandwiched into the gap between the witches' and demons' districts, heading towards the taller buildings at the far end of the town.

She looked down at his hand on her arm, burning where he touched.

Did he burn for her too?

She wasn't sure anymore.

After their first explosive night, they had passed several days in his house in London. He had spent every waking hour of their time together with his head deep in his books or questioning her about Marius, gathering every single detail, no matter how small. She had tried to be patient, because she wanted Marius off her tail, but with every second they had been together, it had been harder to resist her growing need for another taste of Owen.

There had been a few times when he had looked as if he wanted her too, burned with a need for her as she burned for him, but nothing had happened.

Other than Owen falling asleep.

After the first time he had dropped into a deep sleep on her, he had explained that it was one of the side effects of his salve. It used his energy as a catalyst to heal him faster, draining him and leaving him tired.

The research wasn't helping matters either. No amount of caffeine had managed to keep her awake after just thirty minutes of reading one of his tomes about cat shifter species. She wasn't sure how he managed to read them for several hours straight without falling into a coma.

They hadn't made love again, but he had kissed her. Well, she had kissed him when he had returned from a trip into the city with basic necessities for her. Make-up not included, much to her chagrin. She had been so glad to see the toothbrush, razor, deodorant and perfume, and a change of underwear or two, that she had kissed him.

Owen had responded deliciously, yanking the plastic bag out of her hand and tugging her into his arms. He had pinned her between his hard body and the wall of his living room and had kissed her.

Really kissed her.

It had been raw with passion, fierce with desire, and had turned her insides molten with need. He had been on the verge of taking things further when her cursed mind had launched her need to shower, shave and make herself a little more presentable at her. She had broken away from him and he had reluctantly let her go when she had told him she needed to freshen up.

When she had come back to the living room, ready to ride him to Hell and back, he had been sitting at his desk, bent over it and sound asleep.

She hadn't had the heart to wake him.

Cait stole a glance at his profile and heat filled her, pushing her into pulling him to face her and kissing him. His injuries were healed now and he hadn't been wearing himself out with research today. Maybe they could find a quiet place to tango before he met his contact.

It was on the tip of her tongue to suggest that when they made it beyond the crush of people that circulated around the largest streets and he released her wrist. Cold instantly settled where his hand had been and she rubbed at her wrist, trying to chase it from her skin.

"Owen?" she whispered, wanting him to look at her so she could gauge his mood before putting voice to her desire.

He glanced across at her. "Almost there."

His smile hit her hard and her knees might have wobbled a little. She pretended not to notice. She wasn't a little kitten, all green and new to desire. Plenty of handsome men had made her the centre of their attention. Owen wasn't the first.

He was the first to shake her world though, rocking her confidence and filling her with an unsettling eagerness, a need she found difficult to deny. He was the first male to make her want to be the centre of his attention.

He was the first male to make her crave his eyes on her alone, his touch reserved for her, and his smiles under her sole possession.

They had to cross another busy thoroughfare and his hand claimed her wrist, sending an electric thrill buzzing through her bones.

Where was he taking her?

Cait hoped it wasn't to the buildings at the far end. It was dangerous around there. Many shifter species had set up packs and dens there, and she had heard they were always at war with each other. There were ogres there too, among other less savoury species.

She eyed the gaudy four storey red building ahead of her, tucked between a building with the banner of a local wolf shifter pack streaming down one of its walls and a building with a banner she didn't recognise.

Several women draped themselves over the balconies on the red building, dressed in minimal clothing and waving at the males below, catching their attention and no doubt their wallets in the process.

Succubi.

Cait never had liked the vixens. They had no morals. Any male was fair game to them. They were worse than the incubi. At least the male sex demons had rules.

Owen released her when they stepped out into a broad street that curved around the taller buildings, running in a sweeping arc that followed their shape and that of the cavern.

"Well if it isn't the handsome Owen Nightingale." A sweet voice sing-songed from above and Cait's hackles rose as she sought the owner and found her.

The dazzling succubus leaned over a balcony on the first floor of the bordello, her large breasts nearly falling out of her skimpy black dress and a smile on her painted red lips as she twirled ash blonde wavy hair around her finger.

Owen raised his hand and smiled at the succubus.

Cait managed to bite back the growl that rumbled up her throat but failed to resist the need to glare at the woman for daring to steal Owen's attention and a smile from him.

"What are you doing in this part of town, Handsome?" The female persisted and Cait wanted to leap up to the balcony, an easy feat for her, and claw the smile off her face.

"Here on business," Owen replied and the succubus finally looked at Cait.

One pale eyebrow rose and she gave Cait a look that left her feeling that she thought Owen could do better.

Cait took a sharp step towards the bordello, her black claws emerging and her vision brightening as her eyes changed, burning with blue fire.

The succubus shrank back from the stone balustrade of the balcony, warily eyeing Cait before disappearing inside.

Owen looked back over his shoulder at Cait, the black slashes of his eyebrows drawn low over his green eyes.

She ignored him and kept walking, passing him and stomping ahead as she wrestled with her feelings, struggling to get them back under her control. She didn't want to delve into why the succubus paying attention to Owen had riled her, but then she didn't need to in order to know that she had been jealous.

Still was jealous.

Cait looked over at Owen as he fell into step beside her, taking in every inch of his six-foot-four athletic frame and how his black button-down shirt stretched snugly across his chest, revealing a hint of his muscles, and how his black jeans hugged his lithe legs. His pale green eyes slid her way and she didn't have time to avert hers before his locked with them, a questioning edge to them.

"Do you often like to pay for your pleasure?" she snapped before she could get the better of herself.

His left eyebrow shot up and then a slow smile spread across his handsome face. He looked back towards the bordello and waved at the succubus again, who had evidently re-emerged from her hiding place.

Cait scowled at him and then at the bitch.

"She paid me."

Those words leaving Owen's lips whipped her gaze back to him.

His wicked mouth curved into a sultry smile.

Cait's flattened into a harsh line.

Owen chuckled. "I did a job for her."

He walked on ahead of her when she stopped dead, cursing herself for not having thought of that. He knew this town well, and everyone here seemed to know him too, even some of the more dangerous characters. It stood to reason that he would have done business here, assisting any number of the people who made this place their home.

But she had jumped straight to the conclusion that he had slept with the female.

What was wrong with her?

Owen stopped and looked back at her. "Keep up and keep your head down. We don't want people discovering what you are in this area of town. Okay?"

She nodded and hurried to catch up with him. During the drive to the beautiful country estate above the fae town, he had told her the same thing on repeat, stating several times that it was important that they get in, see what information they could discover about Marius from Owen's contact, and get out without rousing suspicion about her. He wanted to protect her. Not only from word spreading about her being there and reaching the male through the grapevine, but from mercenaries in the town who worked for the black markets.

Owen had told her that he didn't want her to end up in their hands.

It had touched her, but he didn't have to worry.

She had no intention of ending up in one of their cages. She was going to keep her head down and let Owen conduct his business, acting as his assistant, and then she was going to make him leave this place. She had enjoyed fae towns once, before meeting Owen.

The things he had told her about them and how many of the people visiting them trafficked in shifters and other species, had changed her view of them.

She wanted to get out as soon as possible and in one piece.

Owen seemed to want to challenge that desire by dragging her to the shifters.

If he had told her before that he was going to bring her to this end of the town, she would have flatly refused to go with him. The concerned look he shot across at her said that he had known that and it was the reason he hadn't mentioned where in the fae town they had been heading.

"It'll be okay," he said, his deep voice curling around her and soothing her nerves. "Just stay close."

He held out his hand to her and she slipped hers into it. Surprise claimed her when he linked their fingers, locking their hands together, his palm pressed against hers.

Cait stared down at their joined hands, struggling to remember the last time a male had held hers. He felt warm and strong against her, and it was comforting. She was stunned that something so simple could give her so much comfort and reassurance. It gave her confidence too. In him. In herself. It restored her balance, as if his strength and calmness was flowing through his hand and into hers, sharing it with her.

"You okay?" Owen said and she lifted her gaze to his, and blinked when she found his green eyes were soft and warm, dazzling her and making her feel light and airy inside.

She nodded.

He smiled, knocking the wind from her, and jerked his chin towards the road ahead of them. "Come on... quicker I get this done... quicker we can get out of here."

She nodded again, wanting that more than anything.

She wasn't afraid of the demons or the succubi, or even the mercenaries that roamed the streets. None of them scared her, but what stood ahead of her did.

She looked there, towards a tall haphazard blue building with a cerulean and silver banner hanging on the wall. Tiger shifters. Beyond their building was a cream one with a black banner. She wasn't familiar with it, but the smell of cat shifters was strong in that direction, a mixture of panther, leopard and lion.

It held an underlying note of hellcat.

Owen headed straight towards that building and the ominous feeling brewing in the pit of her chest grew with each step and each hard breath she sucked down into her lungs as she fought for air.

The male wasn't here.

She knew that.

But a hellcat was and that meant the meeting that Owen had set up was about to go any way other than how he expected it.

Each step closer she got to the cream building, the hairs on the back of her neck rose higher and her claws grew longer. She curled her free hand into a fist to conceal them, digging them into her palm as she fought for calm and for control.

The deep primal instinct beating in her heart made having that control impossible.

It drove her to fight.

Owen glanced back at her when she dug her claws into the back of his hand, a flicker of concern in his green eyes.

"You sure you're okay?" he said and turned towards her, his gaze searching hers, filled with warmth that soothed her a degree and gave her the strength to nod.

She could keep control of herself. Her will was stronger than her instincts.

She could keep control.

Owen began walking again and a big tawny-haired male with bright golden eyes stepped out from the cream building, flanked by two other males of similar stature and breadth.

"Niko?" Owen said and the brute nodded.

Cait sniffed and rubbed her nose, pretending there was something wrong with it as she tried to catch Niko's scent.

He smelled like a panther, but mingled with his scent was that of another.

Hellcat.

Her claws grew further and her fangs began to descend, the drive to break free of Owen's grip and shove past the male to burst into the building almost seizing control of her. She breathed slowly and deeply, focusing on Owen's hand and how good it felt as it clutched hers, using him to keep herself rooted to the spot. She didn't want to fight.

"I'm Owen." He held his free hand out to the shifter but the male only looked at it. "I contacted you about needing some information."

Niko nodded and folded his arms across his broad muscular chest, causing the tight white t-shirt he wore with his dark blue jeans to stretch even tighter across his biceps. His golden gaze slid towards Cait, briefly narrowed, and then edged away again.

Cait mentally bared her fangs at him.

Owen's plan was a bust.

This male knew what she was because he was involved with one of her kind. He could smell it on her, just as she could smell female hellcat all over him.

Her fangs punched longer, the lower canines growing to match the upper ones as her instincts began to hijack her body, bending her to their will.

"I don't like how she smells," the male to the left of Niko grumbled and the one beside him nodded, flicking a glance at her, and then a glare at Owen.

"I don't like him either. What's a hunter want with us?"

"I'm not here for you. I'm not even here to speak with you." Owen lifted the flap on his black satchel and took his tablet device out. He flipped the cover open and managed to swipe the screen without releasing her hand.

Cait was thankful for that as he turned the device towards Niko. Could Owen sense how close to the edge she was? If he let go of her hand, she wouldn't be able to stop herself from launching past the panther shifter and seeking out the hellcat.

She needed to fight.

The urge was overwhelming, built into all females of her species. They were highly territorial, driven to battle each other whenever they crossed paths, both for the sake of expanding their territory and for the sake of having the attention of more males.

It was a stupid instinct. Cait had always hated it. Modern female hellcats were neither interested in territory nor males. It was the reason the males had taken to enslaving them.

"Seen this guy around?" Owen said as he showed the tablet screen to Niko.

The big panther shifter's eyes narrowed and he nodded. "He was here about a week ago, but I've seen him before that. I know what he is."

Owen's hand tensed in hers but it was the only sign that he had stiffened on hearing that the panther knew the male in question was a hellcat. His schooled expression and casual demeanour concealed everything she could sense in him through their linked hands. It had shaken him.

Because of her.

He feared that the panther knew what she was, and he was right to fear it, because Niko did know. His minions didn't though. They appeared to have blunter senses, which made Cait suspect the pair were of a weaker cat shifter species, possibly lion. Male lions had dull senses, because they relied heavily on their harem of females for hunting and protection.

They were lazy and filled with conceited pride and a sense of entitlement, just like male hellcats.

Cait sneered at them.

The one to Niko's left glared at her and bared his fangs. "I don't like the bitch."

Niko ignored the male and studied the tablet Owen was holding out to him, his golden eyes swiftly darting across the screen as he read the information Owen had gathered so far on the male hellcat.

The lion males exchanged a glance.

All hell broke loose.

Owen launched himself between her and the two males just as they lunged for her. He took a hard blow to the right side of his jaw, grunted and staggered left before hitting the cobbled street in a slump, his tablet spilling from his hand.

The panther male reached out to grab hold of both of his minions. He snagged one by the collar of his t-shirt and the other evaded him, heading straight for Owen.

Cait leaped between Owen and the male, shielding him with her body, and growled low in her throat.

The change was upon her before she could consider what she was doing, her twin tails sprouting from the base of her spine as black fur coursed over her body. Her ribs expanded and limbs shifted, the violence of the transformation tearing her corset and leather trousers apart. She dropped onto all four paws as she completed the shift and snarled at the three males standing dumbstruck in front of her.

Her tails swished, the blue flames that coated their tips fluttering as she moved them, and she stared down the male who had gone after Owen.

She could feel Owen's intense and focused gaze on her as he picked himself up off the cobbles and could sense his astonishment and awe on her sharper senses.

She looked back at him, blue flames licking around her teeth as she dragged air in over them to catch his scent of spice and fire.

His green eyes widened, his heart pounding in her ears.

Cait turned her focus back on the three shifter males. The panther looked as if he was considering shifting too. If he did, he would be an imperfect mirror of her sleek black form, a weaker version far smaller than she was.

She huffed, the flames flickering around her fangs dancing forwards on the air, and lowered her head. The blue fire that normally engulfed only the last third of her tails spread downwards as her anger rose. Cerulean flames burst from beneath her paws too, twisting and twining up her black legs.

Cait hissed and growled, the strange sound echoing off the buildings around her and drawing too many eyes her way.

Owen had wanted her to keep a low profile.

She hadn't been able to stop herself from changing to protect him and she wasn't sure she could stop herself from attacking the males to make them pay for harming him.

A murmur ran through the crowd gathering around them.

Owen shoved his tablet into his satchel and hissed at her. "Cait."

She looked back at him and he looked off to his left. Her gaze followed his and fear trickled through her when she spotted the three big demons amidst the crowd, swords strapped to their backs and their eyes pinned on her as they talked in low voices.

About her.

Mercenaries.

Shit was about to go even further south.

CHAPTER 7

Owen grabbed Cait's hand the second she had finished transforming back into her normal form. He ran with her, shoving through the narrowest point in the crowd and then dragging her down a side street. She looked back over her shoulder, sure the three demons were following, and gasped when she spotted them lumbering towards her.

Cait wrapped her free arm across her chest to cover her breasts and ran harder, sprinting alongside Owen as he blazed a trail through the fae town, his satchel bouncing against his hip. He knew it better than she had thought, or he was just running in a crazy pattern to throw the demons, because he kept twisting and turning down smaller and smaller alleyways.

Slowing the demons down.

The males were mostly mortal in appearance, with the exception of the dusky ridged horns that curled from behind the tops of their pointed ears, and their impressive stature. All of them stood several inches taller than Owen and all were at least twice his breadth. The smaller alleys made their pursuit difficult as they tried to squeeze their big muscular bodies down the narrow gaps between the buildings.

Cait was beginning to see how Owen had survived so long as a hunter. He was resourceful and a quick thinker. He knew his opponents weaknesses and took full advantage of them.

And he knew when to beat a fast retreat.

The demons were further behind now, but she wasn't sure how long it would last. Demons could teleport and they could fly, and she had no doubt they would use that to their advantage now their prey was breaking away from them.

Owen broke out onto one of the main cobbled streets, eliciting shocked gasps from the people he nearly mowed down.

Cait elicited several stares, mostly from the males. Some of their females noticed and cuffed them around the back of their heads. She didn't have a chance to apologise to the women for her state of undress. Owen yanked her with him, but not down another side street as she had expected.

He pulled her at a rapid pace down the main street.

Heading towards the witches' district.

Cait shook her head. Bad move. They were being chased by demons and witches were more likely to drive them out than let them in when they had trouble of that magnitude on their heels.

The storeowners ahead of them seemed to get wind of them coming and the street suddenly cleared, all of the patrons melting into the alleys as the witches came out from their shops. Her eyes widened as more appeared, most of the women wearing the traditional plain black dress of a witch on duty. They formed a line across the street, blocking the way, and the electric sizzle of magic charged the air.

She tugged on Owen's hand, trying to drag him towards the last available side street.

His hand clenched hers, a vice-like grip she couldn't shake, and he flicked a smile at her that she guessed was meant to be reassuring.

It wasn't.

In front of them was a blockade of witches who all felt ready to launch a violent spell, and behind were a group of enormous demons charging like a herd of enraged Hell beasts.

Rock and a hard place came to mind.

She almost wanted to close her eyes as Owen approached the witches at full speed, his boots pounding the cobbles, afraid they were about to collide. She did flinch as they reached the blockade and then her eyebrows shot up as they breezed straight through the witches.

Cait looked back in time to see the gap that had opened in the blockade close behind them and the witches launch the spells she had sensed, aiming them all at the demons.

A young brunette witch came running at them, waving frantically. "Owen!"

Cait stared at the pretty little thing. "Did you do a job for her too?"

"No." The hardness of his tone warned she wouldn't get anything other than that out of him, but it didn't stop her from wanting to press and see if she could.

"This way." The witch twisted on the spot in a move that had to have been made possible by magic and zoomed down a side street to Cait's right.

Owen skidded on the cobbles, swiftly changing direction, and dragged Cait with him as he pounded down the alley behind the witch. Each hard stride hurt Cait's bare feet, the cobbles biting into her bones as she landed awkwardly on them every time, seemingly doomed to land all of her steps wrongly. She wanted to slow down but Owen refused to let her.

He followed the witch through the maze of streets between the white rustic buildings, leaving the stores behind and heading into a residential area.

The petite brunette halted outside a small single-storey rectangular dwelling with an emerald green wooden door and produced an enormous ring of keys from out of thin air. She rifled through them, the keys jangling frantically as she searched for the right one. It set Cait on edge and she looked around them.

A huge bright blue explosion lit the air beyond the houses, back in the direction they had come, and the sulphurous smell of magical discharge drifted down to her.

The witches were still fighting.

Cait didn't have a damned clue what was going on anymore and she wanted an explanation.

The witch finally found the key and unlocked the door. Owen shoved it open and bundled Cait through it, tugging her close to him, the heat of his body and the feel of it pressing against her distracting her for a second, making her forget the insanity that had just happened.

"I left everything as it was for you," the witch said, pulling Cait back to the world.

Owen released Cait and crossed the small living area to a worn black leather armchair set in front of the dark fireplace. He removed his satchel and dumped it onto the chair, grabbed the checked blanket from it and came back to her. His gaze studied her face as he unfurled the blanket, settling it around her shoulders.

"Are you okay?" he husked, the rich deep sound of his voice warming her right down to her bones.

He clutched her shoulders through the blanket and she nodded as she gathered it around herself, holding it closed in front of her chest.

He smiled and she didn't give him a chance to move away from her. She launched a hand out from beneath the blanket and snagged his wrist.

"You lived here... in the witches' district?" Her gaze searched his for the truth, afraid that he would keep it to himself, another of his secrets that stirred her curiosity about him and made her want to pry it from him.

He nodded, but gave her no explanation, just as she had expected.

She released him when the brunette witch approached him and he turned to face the woman, a glimmer of something like affection filling his green eyes. The witch tiptoed and pressed a kiss to his cheek, her deep brown eyes closing in time with his, and Cait wanted to growl at how close they appeared and how both seemed to take comfort from that intimate caress.

The witch set back down on her heels. "It's good to see you again... but don't bring trouble with you next time. Lay low for a few hours. I'll let you know when you're safe to move."

The petite female turned away from Owen and walked towards Cait where she lingered near the door. Her eyes turned dark, narrowing on Cait as she passed, leaving her feeling that the demons weren't the trouble the woman had been speaking about. She thought Cait was trouble.

Cait waited for the door to close before looking at Owen. "I get the feeling your little witch doesn't like me."

His expression remained emotionless and unreadable, his green eyes giving nothing away. No reaction to either of her tests. The witch didn't like her. The witch was Owen's. It was the only conclusion she could draw and it stoked her blood, making it burn again, worse than it had when she had thought the succubus had been in a relationship with Owen.

Cait looked around the cramped house.

It consisted of a small living area that had more books in it than his expansive drawing room back at his house in London and a closed door to another room. She tried to use the time it took her to study the cluttered room to grapple with her emotions and get them back under control, but the fire in her veins refused to simmer down, rolling at a steady boil that had her itching to track down the witch or turn on Owen.

Since tracking down and confronting a witch felt like a dangerous move, she settled on glaring at Owen.

She was starting to hate his secrets.

"Why do you own a place in the witches' district?" she snapped and tossed the blanket he had placed around her shoulders, feeling no need for it now that they were alone.

He had already seen her naked. He had already seen her in her cat form. She had no secrets now, no mystery left. She had already given him what he had desired as payment for the job. There was nothing stopping him from backing out of it and leaving her to deal with the male alone.

Nothing except pride and honour.

She wasn't sure how much of those two things a man with secrets could have.

"Did you share it with the witch?"

Cait hated herself for how that question came out, laced with uncertainty and fear, and a sprinkling of ridiculous hope. What was she doing? What was it about Owen that had her tied in knots? He made her feel weak. He made her feel vulnerable. He stripped away her strength until she felt that all she could do was rely on him, trust in him, and pray to her gods that he wouldn't take that trust and destroy her with it.

Owen frowned at her from across the room, his muscular chest rising and falling with each hard breath he drew, pressing against his snug black shirt. His green eyes darkened a full shade.

He finally shook his head.

"I lived here alone." He took a measured step towards her and she backed away one, feeling uncertain about everything and unwilling to allow him close to her when she didn't know what she was doing or whether she was coming or going.

She wanted to go.

She wanted to stay.

He tore her in too many directions, pulling her apart more and more each hour she knew him. Every instinct she possessed demanded she stay.

With him.

"Does it make you feel better that I lived here alone?" he murmured, a wickedness entering his eyes, leaving her feeling he could see straight through her eyes and down into her soul and her heart, and he knew all of her. Every secret. Every feeling. *Everything.* "If you keep on like this, I might start thinking you're jealous, and then I might just have to ask why."

Cait lowered her gaze to her bare feet, trying to ignore the way he was looking at her, his green eyes filled with hunger again, heat that set her on fire and made her burn.

She didn't move as he approached her but she did lift her head and look over her shoulder when he passed her. She tracked his progress across the room and watched as he locked the door, turned his back to it and leaned against it.

Her heart thudded against her ribs.

Heat pooled lower, settling in her belly.

He wasn't going to let her leave.

Her foolish questions and her weakness had given him control over her, a piece of her she couldn't take back. He knew. She stared at him, her eyes locked with his, heat burning between them and sucking all the air from the room. She couldn't think straight when he was looking at her like that. He looked like a man with an insatiable hunger, one that consumed and controlled him, a need that ran as deep in him as the one that ran through her.

When he looked at her like that, making her feel that she wasn't alone in what she was feeling, and that he felt it too, she wanted to fall into his arms and trust he could see her safely through whatever was happening between them.

Did he feel the same fierce attraction as she did? The same consuming passion? The same intense need that left her feeling she would die if they were separated?

His green gaze narrowed, filling with the heat and hunger that existed inside her, silently answering her questions. He felt it too. She wasn't alone.

"You do seem a little jealous," he husked and canted his head to one side, causing strands of his dark hair to fall down and caress his brow.

She wanted to close the gap between them and brush those strands back, to sweep her fingers across his brow in their place, and then flutter them down to his cheek, stirring the passion that blazed in his eyes until it burned as wild and hungrily as her own.

"First the succubus." He pushed away from the door and slowly prowled towards her. Her breathing hitched, coming quicker as he drew closer, his eyes constantly fixed on hers and holding her immobile. Powerless against his dark allure. "Now my cousin Julianna."

Cait gasped. "Cousin?"

He nodded and the fog of lust and desire cleared from her mind, instantly evaporating as she realised the true depth of what he had just told her. A secret, one he evidently held close to his chest, unwilling to reveal it to anyone.

She had heard a thousand tales of Owen Nightingale and if the world knew what he had just confessed to her, she was sure every one of those tales would have mentioned it.

Owen Nightingale was a witch.

Cait looked up into his eyes as he neared her, his heat and masculine scent swirling around her, completely enclosing her and narrowing the world down to only him.

He lowered his head, looking down into her eyes through ones that held a cold note, an edge that warned he wanted her to say something, needed to hear what she thought of what he had told her.

That alone confirmed her suspicions that he had offered up his secret to her.

It touched her.

"I always felt as if you had cast a spell on me... weaving your black magic from the moment I set eyes on you." She lifted her hand and brushed her knuckles across his cheek, her breath leaving her in a rush as his eyes closed and he leaned into her touch, seeking more from her.

How could he make her feel so weak one moment and so powerful the next?

To have such a male seeking comfort from her, to feel that he needed this from her and only her, empowered her. It felt as if he had just placed something precious into her hands and trusted her not to use it against him.

A male witch. She still couldn't believe it, even when the knowledge of what he was made everything she had felt in him make sense at last. The source of the sensation she had about him, the sense that he was dangerous and powerful despite being mortal, was magic, buried deep in his blood.

"You don't have to be jealous, Cait," he murmured and slowly opened his eyes, raising them to meet hers. They seemed brighter, overflowing with heat and tenderness as they held hers, stealing her breath away and making her heart race. "You were beautiful when you shifted... I mean...

you were even more beautiful. I didn't think it was possible... but you were."

Her eyes widened and he covered the hand she had against his face with his, took hold of it and brought it down between them, holding it close to his chest.

"If anyone has cast a spell, Cait... it was you... you've bewitched me."

CHAPTER 8

Owen felt as if he had just laid his heart on the line as he looked down into Cait's wide blue eyes, his mouth turning impossibly dry as he waited for her to say something. Anything would do. He just needed to break the thick silence that had descended, sucking the air from the small living room.

His heart pounded as he waited, a sickening rhythm that left him feeling weak right down to his marrow. He had faced countless enemies but none of them had been as daunting as facing Cait in this moment.

He cursed himself for saying something so revealing, words that had put a piece of himself out there for her to snatch and hold to her chest, or snatch and crush out of existence.

It had been bad enough when he had started waxing lyrical about her hellcat form, conveying in the most atrocious and schoolboy sounding way that he had been amazed by the sight of her, stunned by how incredibly beautiful she had been.

Her black fur had been glossy and she had been larger than a panther in size, and her form had been more lithe and sleek. Her twin tails had astounded him, the way blue fire had flickered from their tips mesmerising him together with how she had breathed that same fire as if it was air.

When she had bared her fangs, the flames dancing around her teeth and fanning outwards on her breath, he had wondered whether he had been dreaming. In all the tales he had heard of hellcats, none had painted a picture that had lived up to the reality of her.

She had been breathtaking.

But she was even more breathtaking as she stood before him, her face free of make-up to reveal her natural beauty and her luscious curves exposed for his eyes to devour, each toned plane of her naked body setting his heart racing for a different reason, all of his blood rushing south at startling speed.

The past few days with her had been hell. He had tried to act professionally and keep his distance, but resisting the desire that blazed between them had been nigh on impossible and he had caved when she had kissed him. That kiss had opened the floodgates, sending need sweeping through him like wildfire, burning away his restraint. Heck, if she hadn't mentioned needing to shower, he would have taken her right there in his living room, up against the wall.

The brief time apart had been enough for the pain meds and his salve to kick in though, making him drowsy and extinguishing his desire as his energy leached from him.

He wasn't sure he could maintain his distance any longer, or that there was any point in denying himself what he wanted—her, pressed against him, wrapped around his body as he made love with her.

She stepped towards him, a measured one that made his breath hitch, and his eyes searched hers again, seeking something from her even though he wasn't sure what it was that he wanted to see.

A glimmer of affection?

Something that would make him feel he wasn't alone as he plummeted, falling hard for her?

His desire began to falter again, allowing fear to sweep back in, vicious words taunting him in his head, telling him that he had moved too quickly and had risked everything for nothing. It was all going to backfire on him.

Now the whole world would know that he was a witch, given that power by his mother.

Only she and his cousin Julianna had known that he had magic in his blood. Everyone else believed that it hadn't passed to him.

Because it shouldn't have.

The magic should have rejected him, as his mother and father had expected, because of his lineage. Previous Nightingales had fallen for witches, and none of the offspring from their unions had borne magic.

Everyone had believed he had been born the same, and he had been. He had exhibited no signs of power in his childhood. It had been during his transition into adulthood when it had appeared and he had been away from the Nightingale family home at the time, here in this fae town with his mother and Julianna.

His mother had feared his father and grandfather would force him to learn dangerous spells so they could use the portals to Hell and hunt bigger targets. She had convinced him to hide his magic from the Nightingale side of his family and had begun to train him in secret.

Owen had feared as his mother had. He had been young, but he had known in his heart that his family would seek to use him as a weapon if they discovered his ability.

He had hidden it from the world, never leaving any witnesses alive, ensuring none knew of the power that ran in his veins.

But he had told Cait.

It had felt right to tell her, to share the secret with her and lift some of the weight from his shoulders. His magic had always weighed heavily on him, because it had always forced him to keep his distance from everyone. It had forced him to live alone, partly because he had believed he would have to continue to keep that secret from whomever he chose to share his life with, and partly out of fear that if that person discovered his power, it would come between them and drive them apart.

And then that person would tell the world.

He had grown weary of holding such an important part of himself back though, locking it away where no one could see it, afraid that he would become a weapon should anyone learn of it.

His family were gone and he was clinging to a ridiculous fear.

And he was tired.

And falling in love with a beautiful woman, one he didn't want to have secrets from, because secrets were dangerous and he didn't want to lose her because he had been too afraid to take the risk and trust her. He didn't want to bring her into his life only for her to discover what he was several years down the line and hate him for never telling her.

She deserved to know everything about him, because she had been honest and open about herself.

She took another step towards him, her blue eyes softening as they searched his. Her rosy lips parted as she stepped closer, narrowing the gap between them, and tilted her head back to keep her gaze on his.

He swallowed hard, a feeble attempt to settle his nerves, and his eyebrows furrowed as he stared down into her eyes, willing her to say something.

She didn't speak.

She slowly lifted her right hand and cupped his cheek, her expression shifting to mirror his, her fine dark eyebrows furrowing as she gazed upon him with warmth, understanding and a flicker of gratitude in her eyes.

When she finally found her voice, her words snatched the piece of his heart he had offered to her and left him feeling it was in good hands.

"You've bewitched me too, Owen Nightingale... and I'm not sure there's a cure for how you make me feel... I'm not sure I would want it even if there was." She smiled when he lowered his head, leaning into her warm palm, stealing every drop of reassurance she was offering him. "I've never met a man like you... I've never met someone who makes me feel like you do."

Owen narrowed his gaze on her and exhaled hard, his nostrils flaring as he caught the heat in her gaze, the desire that burned fiercely in his heart too, born of an attraction that ran deeper than blood and bone. It filled his soul and told him to seize hold of her and never let her go.

She had been made for him.

He felt certain of that.

This beautiful woman standing before him, her blue eyes overflowing with warmth and passion, and honesty, had been created solely for him.

She was the one he had been waiting his entire existence to meet.

The only one he would surrender his heart to.

He claimed her bare hips with his hands and pulled her closer to him, his gaze fixed on hers, his breathing coming quicker as she pressed her hands to his chest. His heart pounded against them, a frantic and wild beat that had his blood thundering in his veins, on fire with a deep need of her.

She tilted her head back, her lips parting in an invitation he was quick to take, dropping his head and seizing them in a fierce kiss that softened as he gathered her into his arms. Her bare skin was warm beneath his palms as he wrapped his arms around her and clutched her ribs, pinning her against him. His body stirred again, the fire of his passion for her roaring back into life as he kissed her and she melted into him, giving control over to him.

Owen groaned when she ran her hands up his chest, clutched the black material of his shirt, and rubbed herself against him. She broke away from his lips, each soft puff of her breath across his face filling him with a powerful urge to lay claim to them again, stoking his hunger for her higher, until he burned so hot he couldn't think straight. He could only feel.

Cait stroked her hands over his chest and then shoved them upwards, grabbing his shoulders and then his neck, dragging him back down to her. She kissed him hard and then broke away again, panting against his lips.

"Please say you have a bedroom in this place."

Heck, he didn't need a bedroom for what he had planned, but his beautiful little kitty was asking for one and he would give her anything she wanted.

He bent at the knee and scooped her up into his arms, one beneath her knees and the other around her back. She mewled and wrapped her arms around his neck and kissed him again, shattering his focus. He walked straight into one of his armchairs and grunted as his left knee struck it hard. Cait giggled.

Owen scowled at her but she showed no sign of repenting.

She kissed him again, softer this time, each brief caress stirring heat and light inside him, until he felt sure he was floating across the room rather than walking.

He finally reached the door to his bedroom and kicked it open, breaking the latch. He swallowed Cait's gasp in a kiss as he carried her inside the small bedroom and refused to let her break away from him as she pressed her palms against his chest. He gathered her closer, kissing her deeper until he had crossed the short distance to the double bed.

He would thank Julianna later for keeping everything in his place in good shape, sparing him from having to break his moment with Cait to beat the dust off the deep crimson bedclothes. It would hardly have been romantic and definitely would have spoiled the mood.

Owen pressed one knee into the mattress and kept kissing Cait as he lowered her onto the bed, covering her with his body. She rubbed her hands over his back as he held his weight off her, balancing on his elbows, and made a short noise of frustration. She tugged at his black shirt.

He was about to break away to remove it for her when the sound of cotton ripping filled the quiet room, her claws making fast work of destroying his best shirt. He frowned as he pulled back and she smiled, an apologetic edge to it that he couldn't bring himself to believe because only mischief shone in her blue eyes.

She tugged at the remains of his shirt, yanking it off him and tossing it away. He went to dip to kiss her again but she ran her hands over his chest, her eyes darkening as she followed each move they made. He groaned and held himself above her on his palms, enjoying her slow exploration and how she looked ready to devour him. The desire in her eyes was enough to send his male pride soaring and he wanted to have her looking at him like that, as if he was gorgeous and she couldn't get enough of him, when he was naked.

Owen rose onto his knees and dropped onto his feet at the edge of the bed.

Cait pushed herself up onto her elbows, her hungry gaze roaming over his body, slowly drifting down it towards his hips. The soft pink tip of her tongue poked out and she ran it across her lower lip, her gaze turning hooded as he reached for his belt.

"Slowly," she whispered, a wicked murmur that made his cock jerk in his black jeans.

Heck, he would do whatever she wanted, was a slave to her as she lay on his bed, naked and beautiful and looking as hungry as he was.

He had never intentionally stripped for anyone before, and he couldn't help wondering how many more firsts Cait was going to steal from him.

He slowly unbuckled his black leather belt, clutched one end and pulled it from the loops of his jeans. Her eyes followed it, the sultry edge to them speaking of wicked thoughts and stirring his imagination. He had never been one for kinky, but fuck he could do kinky for her. He had an undeniable urge to use the belt to secure her somehow, but feared how she would react, his mind darting back over everything she had said to him about hellcat males believing the females were there to service them.

The last thing he wanted was her believing he was like them, liable to try to confine and control her. Her spirit and wildness was part of her allure for him and he had no interest in taming her.

She held her left hand out to him, palm up, her eyes on his.

Owen placed his belt into it and his heart thudded as she eyed it and then him.

If she wanted restraints, he could knock up something using magic, but it would probably take a while and he didn't want the moment to fade away, the mood to disappear as he worked.

"Not this time, Little Kitty," he purred and popped the first button on his black jeans.

Her left hand fell, the belt forgotten as her eyes leaped back to him, locked with intent on his hands. She devoured everything he gave to her, each slow slide of a button through a hole and each inch further his fly opened. Her throat worked on a hard swallow when he went to part his fly and reveal himself, and she scowled when he didn't, closing it again and ensuring she didn't get a glimpse.

"You're a tease, Owen Nightingale." She huffed and he toed his boots off, taking his time about it even when he wanted to rush.

She had told him to undress slowly after all.

He kicked his boots aside and moved his hands back to his jeans, regaining her attention. Her pupils expanded, gobbling up the bright blue of her irises as they began to glow around their centres. He was coming to love it when her eyes did that, burning with cold fire that made him hot all over.

He slowly inched his jeans down his hips and she moaned as his cock sprang free, her gaze fixing on it and darkening, filling with need that echoed within him too. He groaned when she moved on the bed, getting onto her hands and knees and crawling towards him. His gaze drifted down the line of her spine to her bare buttocks, watching them as they shifted with alluring and sensual grace. He groaned again and dragged his eyes back up, settling them on her face.

Cait's blue eyes leaped up to his and then back to his length.

She stopped at the edge of the bed, hooked her fingers into the pockets of his jeans where they hung around his thighs, and tugged him towards her. He stumbled forwards and could only throw his head back and unleash the moan that burned up his throat as she ran her tongue up the length of his cock.

He jerked when she shoved his jeans down to his knees and moaned when she skimmed her hands up his thighs, pressing her fingers in at times, a brief glimpse of her strength that thrilled him.

Owen felt her gaze on him, burning into his face. He dropped his head and looked down at her, the sight of her kneeling before him, her face level with his shaft, ripping another moan from his throat and making his length kick with eagerness. She smiled wickedly and slowly lowered her gaze to it, her attention only making the need within him spiral higher, until he wasn't sure he could take any more.

"Touch me," he whispered, a plea that he couldn't hold back.

She ran her right hand up his thigh and he shuddered as she cupped his balls, his hips thrusting involuntarily. She moaned and his breath hitched as she leaned in, bringing her sweet lips close to his cock. She teased him, hovering close, her warm moist breath skating over his sensitive flesh.

Heck, he could probably come from just that if she did it for much longer.

Pressure built inside him, an unstoppable force that tore at his control. He ran his left hand over her sleek dark hair, twisted the black strands into his fist, and guided her downwards. Her eyes remained locked on his as she parted her lips and took him inside her mouth, the most erotic thing he had ever seen. He couldn't breathe as she took hold of his length in her right hand, clutching it tightly, and moved on him, taking him deep into her warm, wet mouth before shifting back, sucking as she withdrew. Her tongue swirled around the blunt head, fluttering and teasing before pressing harder against the slit.

Fuck.

His breath left him in a rush and his thighs trembled as she went to war, tearing down his defences, alternating between sucking him and teasing the head, her eyes constantly on his.

He couldn't take it.

He wanted to explode in her mouth, but he needed to be inside her even more than that.

He needed to hear her cry his name as he gave her the release she craved.

His little kitty needed.

He would give her everything she desired.

CHAPTER 9

Cait mewled as Owen tightened his grip on her hair and moved her away from him. She tried to get closer to him again, filled with an overwhelming need to stroke his cock with her tongue, to pleasure him until his legs gave out and he couldn't walk. He refused, his free hand clamping down on her shoulder.

"Next time."

He kept saying that. He kept making her wait, and each time he did, it increased her desire to do whatever he had denied her.

Right now, she wanted to flip him onto his back, tie him to the wooden railings of his headboard, and suck him until he exploded and shouted her name loud enough that everyone in the fae town would know where they were.

He had other ideas.

Ones she could definitely go along with.

He kicked off his black jeans, pushed her onto her back and crawled onto the bed, looming over her, his length jerking between them. She went to run her hand down it but he caught her wrist and pinned it to the crimson covers above her head. The dark look in his eyes sent a hot shiver through her and she melted beneath him, surrendering with only the slightest of struggles, just enough to fire him up and fire her up with him.

She wriggled, pretending to fight his hold, and his green gaze darkened two more shades, the black chasms of his pupils speaking of his arousal as much as the hard heavy length between them.

She reached for it with her other hand.

Owen scowled and caught that hand too, pinning it above her head with the other one. The action forced him down into contact with her and he hissed, his face screwing up in pleasure as she rocked against him, rubbing his shaft.

He breathed harder as she kept up her rubbing, pushing him to see what he would do. She could sense the battle in him, the internal war he waged, torn between letting her grind against him and dragging himself away. He was close, she knew that, had felt it when she had been sucking him. Would he win the battle and find the strength to pull away, or would he surrender and spill onto her stomach?

He was stronger than she had thought.

He grunted and shoved back, bringing his knees up between her thighs to lift him beyond her reach. She moaned and tried to reach him anyway, angling her body and pressing her feet into the mattress to raise her hips off the bed.

He evaded her, a wicked smile on his profane lips.

"Need me there?" he husked, his deep voice thick with desire, arousal that shone in his hooded green eyes as he looked down at her.

She nodded. "Gods, yes."

He grinned, a cocksure one that made her heart leap even when she knew it shouldn't. There was male pride in that smile, masculine satisfaction that she found strangely alluring. She liked seeing Owen like this, sure of himself, filled with confidence and strength. She liked that she was the one who made him feel that way.

Because he made her feel that way too.

Being with him, catching the way he gazed at her whenever he thought she wasn't looking, as if she was the centre of the universe and made it spin for him, and the way he looked at her when he knew she was looking, as if he would die if he didn't get a taste of her and thought she was beautiful, filled her with strength and confidence.

It filled her with the feeling that she could let her guard down around him and place her trust in him, and he would never do anything to make her regret it.

He lowered his head and kissed her, a brief hard clash of their lips that lasted barely a few seconds before he was moving on. His hands claimed her hips and he pushed her upwards across the dark red covers as he moved downwards, kissing a trail down her chest. She moaned and arched into him as he wrapped his lips around her left nipple, tugging the aching bead into his mouth, sending sparks skittering across her skin.

He thumbed her other nipple, causing the fiery sparks to sweep outwards from that one too. They collided above her heart and filled it with fire that drifted downwards in time with Owen, heading towards her belly. He trailed his lips over her skin, kissing the underside of her breast before moving on, placing wet open mouth kisses down the centre of her stomach. She moaned and wriggled, eager for him to head to where she needed him, just as he had promised.

His hands tightened against her hips again and he pushed her further up, until her head almost came off the edge of the bed. He placed a kiss on the triangle of curls that covered her mound and then eased her thighs apart. His moan filled the room and sent another scorching wave of heat through her. She couldn't stop herself from looking at him, driven to see the expression on his face as he stared down at her hips. There was such hunger in it, such fierce passion and need.

"Owen," she whispered, breathless with need herself.

The right corner of his mouth quirked and he lowered his head, closed his eyes and gave her what she wanted.

She cried out with the first stroke of his tongue over her sensitive flesh and shuddered in bliss with the second, the fire in her belly igniting into an inferno he stoked by skimming his fingers down the length of her. She threw her arms above her head, clutched the covers that hung over the side of the bed, and arched off the mattress as he slid two fingers into her, a prelude that only made her want the main act even more.

She craved the feel of him inside her, filling and stretching her, completing her in a way that she would never stop needing.

He pumped her slowly with his fingers, rubbing the flats of them over her sweet spot as he stroked her with his tongue, teasing her nub and sending waves of blistering fire burning through her. She tossed her head to one side and bit her lip as she moaned, his assault too much to bear, pushing her too swiftly to the edge. She fought it, wanting to draw out the pleasure of his mouth on her and his fingers thrusting into her core.

Her body had other ideas, flexing around his fingers, clenching him as it overrode her head and sought release.

Owen groaned and licked her harder before suckling her, drawing her aroused bead into his mouth and wreaking havoc on her.

She cried out and he thrust his fingers deeper, ripping a second moan from her lips. She clutched the covers, her claws tearing into the material as she rocked against his face, too lost now to control herself. Release came upon her in a brutal wave, battering her and sweeping her away, sending white-hot shivers blazing down her legs and up her torso as she convulsed against Owen's wicked mouth and cried his name.

His movements slowed, fingers pumping at a leisurely pace as he kissed her between her thighs, bringing her down from her high but not releasing her. She was too sated to move, her bones liquid beneath her skin. She lay at his mercy, hazy and high.

Arousal began another slow build within her as the haze of her first climax subsided, Owen's fingers working their magic as he coaxed her and teased her. Each sweep of his lips across her sensitive nub had her shivering with aftershocks of pleasure. Each one had her steadily soaring towards her next release.

When she gave in to the urge to rock on his fingers again, he withdrew them from her and placed one last kiss to her mound before rising over her. The wicked hunger in his dark green gaze stole her breath away and she had to fight for air as he claimed her hips and pulled her closer to him, dragging her across the bed.

She twined her fingers in her black hair, keeping her gaze locked on his, her legs spread and welcoming him. She wanted him inside her now, his long length filling her, bringing her to another shattering release.

His eyes darkened further and he dropped them to her body, running them down the length of her to her hips. She moaned when he fisted his cock, stroking it hard, revealing the moisture-tipped crown. She reached for him, wanting to run her hand down his length and brush her fingers through his dark curls to cup his balls.

Owen met her hand with his, pressed the tips of their fingers together, and then slid his between hers, closing them over the back of her hand. He locked their hands together and leaned forwards, coming to pin her hand beside her shoulder and bringing his face above hers.

He stared down at her, the intensity in his gaze thrilling her, stirring her need for him to dazzling heights.

He took hold of her free hand and she thought he meant to pin that too, but he surprised her by bringing it down between them and settling it around his shaft. He curled his hand over hers and moved it on him, giving the act of stroking him a new highly arousing state. She liked how he guided her, gripping her hand tightly, making her touch him.

"Cait," he breathed, his eyes fluttering closed, and she knew what he needed.

She eased him downwards and he did as she instructed, shifting his hips back and down, bringing them closer. She ran the head of his length between her wet folds and he groaned, the husky sound of it eliciting one of her own. She would never tire of hearing Owen's pleasure as they came together.

He released her hand and planted his onto the mattress beside her hip, holding himself off her as she guided him downwards. The head of him nudged into her sheath and he swallowed hard, opened his eyes and stared down into hers as she took her hand away. He eased into her, slowly and steadily, drawing out the union. When he was fully sheathed, he clutched her hand and pinned it in the same way as her other one, and began moving inside her.

Each long slow withdraw and deep unhurried thrust had her clutching his hands, pressing her black claws into the backs of them. He claimed her lips with a soft kiss that left her feeling he was stealing more than her breath from her.

He was stealing her heart.

She had expected hot and fierce, as they had been during their first time. This slow, passionate moment building between them was too much for her, stripping away all of her defences and leaving her bare. She kissed him back, mirroring his softness and tenderness, lost in how good it felt to have him slowly filling her, reaching every part of her and leaving all of her touched by this moment with him.

She moaned in time with him as he began to quicken the pace, his hips flexing and driving him deeper. The feel of his powerful body against hers tore another moan from her lips, making her want to run her hands over him and feel how each muscle bunched and flexed as he made love with her.

His kiss grew heated, his tongue demanding entrance that she granted. She eagerly tackled it with her own, stroking the length of his tongue and eliciting a groan from him. He moved deeper and harder, his tempo increasing as the heat within her built back towards a crescendo, each long drive of his cock sending her soaring higher.

"Owen," she murmured against his lips and he grunted, released one of her hands and gave her what she desired, as if he could sense it inside her, knew her so well already that he could read her needs.

He clutched her hip and thrust harder, and she drifted her hand over his shoulder, moaning as she kissed him and felt his muscles shifting beneath her palm, each powerful flex of his body thrilling her.

"Cait," he whispered and grunted as he pressed his forehead against hers and then shifted to one side.

His breath was hot on her throat as he rocked into her, his skin slick with sweat beneath her hand. She moaned and he tightened his grip on her other hand, digging his fingertips into her. His other hand held her hip, pinning her in place as he moved inside her, each powerful thrust rocking her.

She opened her eyes and pressed the side of her head against his, moaning as he dropped his mouth to her throat and kissed it.

Need blazed through her, hot and fierce, burning away everything and leaving only instinct behind.

That powerful need beat in her blood and drummed in her heart, pounding in her head until she was a slave to it, unable to deny it any longer even when a tiny sliver of her knew that she had to stop herself.

She couldn't.

As Owen plunged deep into her, his lips devouring her throat, she surrendered to that dark and consuming need.

She plunged her fangs into the left curve of his neck.

Owen lifted his head and cried out, his body shuddering against hers as she sank her fangs deeper. Her entire body quaked as the first drops of his blood hit her tongue and she came alive as she swallowed the coppery potent liquid flowing into her mouth. Fire and lightning blazed through her veins and she gave a muffled cry as Owen grunted, thrust deep into her and came, her own release chasing his as he spilled inside her, his length throbbing and his body trembling violently.

Heat shimmered through her and bliss rode in its wake, a heady and intoxicating high that left her shaking all over.

Owen sagged against her.

The heat inside her turned as cold as ice and her ecstasy became agony as what she had done dawned on her.

She wrenched her fangs from his throat and quickly licked the twin puncture marks, a ridiculous part of her believing that it would somehow fix the mess she had made.

It wouldn't.

What had she done?

He would never forgive her.

He would never love her.

He would hate her.

Because she had just sentenced him to an agonising death.

CHAPTER 10

Cait rolled Owen off her, grasped his shoulders and looked down at him. Unconscious. Gods help her. She shook him, silently begging him to wake up and make this nightmare go away. Crimson trailed down from the twin puncture wounds on the left side of his throat, taunting her with reality.

She had bitten him.

"Owen." She shook him harder, tears burning the backs of her eyes as she willed him to respond.

He didn't.

She smoothed her hand across his brow, grimacing as she felt how hot he was already, burning up because of her.

Tears lined her lashes and her eyebrows furrowed as she stroked his paling cheek, fear filling her heart and regret tearing her to pieces inside.

"Please, Owen," she murmured but he still didn't move.

What had she done?

She should have fought harder for control. She should have remained aware of just how dangerous her bite was.

Hellcats were one of a handful of shifter species who could transmit their abilities to another via blood. Mortals bitten by her kind rarely survived the transition.

A single bite had doomed Owen to death.

She screwed her eyes shut and refused to believe that, unwilling to throw in the towel without a fight. She had done this and she would help him through it somehow, although she wasn't sure how he would react if she did manage to bring him to a point where he regained consciousness.

There was no way of reversing what she had done.

If he survived the assault on his body, the stress of the monumental changes he was about to go through, he would become a hellcat like her.

He had thought her beautiful in her hellcat form, but that hardly meant he had any desire to be one himself.

She pressed her hand against his brow again. It was damp and hot beneath her palm. She needed to get his temperature down somehow.

She shoved off the bed and rushed to the closed door in the wall to the left of the door that led to the living room. She pushed it open and scanned the small bathroom, spotted a hand towel near the white basin, and hurried to wet it under the cold tap. When it was soaked, she wrung it out and raced back to Owen.

Cait kneeled on the bed beside him, rolled the white towel up and placed it across his brow.

She sat back and stared down at him, unsure what else she could do. She had no experience of looking after others and she wasn't sure it would even help. If she was going to save Owen's life, then she needed to find out how other mortals had survived the transition.

She needed help.

Owen suddenly writhed on the bed, kicking at the covers and groaning. She pinned his shoulders to the bed to stop him and silently apologised again when he fought her. Sweat dotted his bare chest and his face. His breathing turned ragged, too fast and shallow for her liking.

She had to do something.

The sound of the front door opening had her rapidly tugging the covers over Owen's lower half and springing from the bed. She rushed to the bedroom door to find his cousin standing in the living room.

"The coast is clear again so you can move about. I brought you some clothes." Julianna turned to face her, raising a plastic bag at the same time. Her arm fell when she set eyes on Cait. "What happened?"

Was it that obvious that something had gone terribly wrong?

Cait touched her lips, realising with dread that it was because she hadn't cleaned her face. Owen's blood still coloured her lips.

And fear coloured her expression.

Cait clutched the doorframe as her knees threatened to give out. "It's Owen."

"What happened to Owen?" The brunette's rich brown eyes flashed dangerously and she stormed towards Cait.

"I bit him... I didn't mean to... maybe I did... it happened so quickly. I couldn't stop myself." Cait stepped aside as Julianna reached her and the witch's eyes landed on Owen and widened as she paled.

When Julianna looked back at her, those same eyes narrowed and darkened, and Cait could feel her power rising, charging the air with an electric current.

"What's it doing to him?"

Cait looked across at Owen. "Turning him like me."

"What are you?"

She glanced at Julianna. "A hellcat."

The petite woman looked as if she wasn't sure what to make of that, or what to say, but Cait could sense the anger in her and could see it in her eyes too.

"I never meant to hurt Owen," Cait whispered and looked back at him, her heart aching as he writhed on the bed, moaning in agony that ripped her apart. "I have to help him somehow."

"How?" Julianna snapped. "Haven't you done enough damage?"

"You don't understand. If I don't help him… he'll die."

Julianna paled again and Cait waited for her to lash out, taking out all of her anger on Cait. She deserved it for what she had done, thoughtlessly condemning Owen to either death or life as a shifter.

The tears on her lashes spilled down her cheeks and she took a wobbly step towards Owen, her eyes locked on him.

"How do you feel about him?" Julianna whispered, capturing Cait's focus and bringing her gaze back to her.

How did she feel about Owen?

Cait had the feeling that if she didn't answer that question honestly, she would be the one not making it out of this small house alive. Julianna looked ready to put an end to her.

She closed her eyes, heaved a sigh, and then lifted her head and forced herself to look at Owen. She allowed every one of her feelings for him to surface, needing to understand them herself, holding none of them back as she sought the answer.

"I think what's happening between us is deeper than just a mutual attraction." Her voice seemed quieter than normal, a bare whisper that didn't sound as if it belonged to her. She felt as if another was speaking and perhaps something else was. Not another person, but another part of her, one she had always guarded. Her heart. "I suspect the reason I bit him is because I couldn't deny a deep primal need that coursed through me… one I'm still vaguely aware of whenever I look at him."

Cait looked across at his cousin, meeting her gaze.

"I think Owen might be my mate… but I'll never find out if that's a possibility unless I save him."

Julianna nodded. "I'll mix up some healing spells to help him… but how are you going to save him?"

Cait didn't know the answer to that question, but she hoped someone in this fae town did.

"There is a female hellcat here… in the shifter quarter. I will ask her." It was dangerous to approach the female but Cait had no choice. She would fight her urge to battle the female for her territory and could only hope that the female would do the same.

"Take the clothes in the bag." Julianna held it out to her and Cait thanked her with an unsteady smile before she looked back at Owen. His cousin touched her arm. "I'll take care of him."

Cait nodded and dragged herself away. Lingering wouldn't help him. Time was of the essence and she wouldn't waste a second.

She pulled on a pair of black jeans that were a little too large for her and a black t-shirt, and fled the house. She sprinted down the alley, tracking

Owen's scent through the streets, using his earthy masculine smell of fire and spice to guide her back to the main thoroughfare. Once she hit it, she sped up, calling on all of her strength and pushing herself to her limit. The cobbles bit into her bare feet but she didn't care this time.

All that mattered was Owen.

She had to reach the shifters and gain an audience with the female hellcat.

It wasn't going to be easy. The two male lions didn't like her and she felt certain that the panther, Niko, felt the same. He would want to protect his female. He would try to stop Cait from reaching the woman.

Cait couldn't let that happen.

The colourful canopies of the witches' district gave way to plain white buildings. Cait moved through the streets with ease, the lower number of people telling her that it was late. Most of the stores she had passed had been closed.

Ahead of her, to the left of the cavern, a three storey black building was bustling with life, a thick gathering of people milling around outside it. A tavern. She spotted several demons among the crowd and ducked down an alley to her right, weaving her way through the narrow streets to avoid being spotted.

The buildings around her were low enough that she could see the looming structures of the shifters' district built into the end of the cavern ahead of her. She scowled at the haphazard blue building that bore the banner of a tiger shifter pride and looked at the one to the left of it. Inside that towering cream building was her only hope of saving Owen.

Cait pushed harder, racing to reach the building, afraid of wasting a single second in case that tiny span of time meant the difference between saving Owen's life and losing him forever.

She broke out onto the broad cobbled street that curved around the end of the cavern, between the lower structures that formed the centre of the town and the tall multi-storey buildings built into the rock around the outside. She didn't slow until she was in front of the arched wooden door of the cream building and banging it down with her fists.

"Open up!" She thumped her hands against the door, rattling it, and a window opened above her to her right.

Cait leaped back and looked there, meeting the gaze of a big tawny-haired male with bright golden eyes. Niko.

"Please... I have to speak with your female." She moved to beneath the male shifter, her heart racing as she stared up at him where he leaned with his elbows on the sill of the window in the second floor, his hands dangling over the edge.

"My female?" His eyebrows crinkled and she silently cursed him for playing dumb.

Her temper frayed, the threads of it snapping as she fought for calm. She was a danger as she was now and this male probably knew it. If she didn't get control of herself, she was liable to give in to the deep instincts blasting through her, commanding her to break into the building and fight the female hellcat.

Cait clenched her fists at her sides and reined in that overwhelming desire.

"I know you have a hellcat in there." She searched his eyes but he gave nothing away.

"Nope. None of your kind here." He held her gaze, unflinching as he spoke that lie.

Bastard.

"I sensed her." She ran her gaze over the cream building, her senses stretching around her and confirming that she had been right and there was a female inside.

Niko's female.

The male was going to lead her in circles in order to protect that female and Cait was wasting precious time.

"Look, I'm not here to fight... I'm here because of Owen. Please..." Cait twisted her hands together and raised her voice, going against all of her better instincts that warned she would be exposing herself if she shouted. It was the only way to get through to this male and possibly his female, and she couldn't hold back her anger any longer. Fear made her reckless. She shouted, "Owen's life is hanging in the balance and I need to find a way to help him through the transition."

Niko's golden eyes widened.

The wooden door creaked open.

"Alice, no!" Niko disappeared from the window but he wasn't quick enough to stop the female hellcat from emerging.

Cait dropped her gaze to the woman as she stood on the step of the building, a ripple of shock flowing through her as she saw the reason why Niko had been so protective of her.

Alice placed slender hands on the large swell of her belly, rubbing it through the rich purple long sleeve maternity top.

No wonder Niko had been protecting her so fiercely. In her condition, she would feel an even stronger need to fight to defend her territory and might end up hurting her unborn cub.

Niko appeared behind her, dwarfing his female, and was in front of her a second later, shielding her with his big body.

Alice peered around his arm at Cait, her pale blue eyes filled with only warmth and compassion, no trace of malice in them. Her sleek black hair fell over her shoulder as she canted her head and smiled.

"It's okay, Niko," Alice said, her soft voice lyrical and light, laced with deep affection.

She stroked Niko's left arm, running one hand up it and over his shoulder, shifting the tight white material of his t-shirt. Niko's golden eyes slid towards his female but he showed no sign of allowing her past him.

Cait backed off a few steps, afraid the compulsion to fight the hellcat for her territory would get the better of her. She didn't want to hurt this female. Alice might be Owen's only hope.

"Niko," Alice murmured, her tone holding a firmer note now. "I must speak with the female and it's a little difficult to do that from back here."

"She'll fight you." Niko practically growled those words, his golden eyes settling back on Cait and brightening as they narrowed.

Cait held her hands up. "I won't. I mean… I don't want to. Have your lion shifters restrain me."

Niko nodded and called over his shoulder. The two males from before appeared and squeezed past him and Alice. They loped over to Cait and seized one arm each, holding her in a vice-like grip that she felt sure she wouldn't be able to break.

The big panther shifter moved to one side to allow Alice past him and then nodded when Alice looked at him. He looped his arms under hers and hooked them over her shoulders, restraining her.

Cait fought the urge to fight as she looked across the narrow strip of cobbles at Alice, breathing as hard as the other female hellcat, her eyes no doubt shining as bright a shade of blue.

"Please… I bit Owen… now I don't know what to do. I was hoping you might." Cait held Alice's vivid blue gaze and relief coursed through her when the other hellcat nodded.

"I saw a male go through a transition once." Those words leaving Alice's lips only made the relief she felt grow stronger, but then the female shattered it by adding, "It was horrendous."

Cait swallowed hard. "What happened?"

"It was close, the male almost died, but in the end what saved him was blood."

Blood.

"Like a transfusion?" Cait searched her eyes, desperate for more information that she could use.

Alice frowned. "He needs to drink yours… it has to come from the hellcat who bit him. The sooner the better. But that isn't all."

A shiver ran down Cait's spine and spread along her limbs when Alice's expression turned cold and serious, laced with unease.

Cait should have known it wouldn't be as simple as just giving Owen blood. She had a horrible feeling that Alice was about to say the last thing she wanted to hear.

"When he's strong enough… you have to force a shift out of him." Alice looked away from her. "It completed the transition I saw… but it almost killed him."

Another cold shiver blasted through Cait like an arctic wind and she struggled to breathe. The thought of forcing her blood down Owen's throat had been sickening enough, but the knowledge that she would have to convince him to shift made her heart feel as if it was splitting in two.

She wasn't sure she had the stomach for it or would be able to convince herself that it was a necessary evil.

Hellcats were different to other cat shifters.

Unlike the other breeds, they could take pain while in their animal form without being forced to shift back into their normal forms.

To force a shift out of a hellcat required pain.

Their defence mechanism was to shift into their stronger form on being badly injured—their cat form.

She had already hurt Owen enough. She didn't want to have to do such a horrific thing to him.

"There's no other way?" she said, and Alice looked across at her, a wealth of sympathy in her blue eyes, and shook her head.

Cait nodded and sucked down a deep breath, struggling to come to terms with what she had to do in order to save Owen's life. He was definitely going to hate her. He would never forgive her when he discovered what she had done to him and what she had put him through.

"Thank you." She managed to smile at Alice and the female nodded. "I wish you well with your pregnancy. The cub is strong. A male."

"A male?" Niko stuttered, his eyes wide and leaping down to Alice as he released her.

Alice shifted to face him and smiled as she touched her swollen belly. "I only just realised it too. It seems the old wives tales about female hellcats having powerful abilities when they group together are true."

Niko placed his hand over Alice's on her stomach and smiled, his golden eyes bright with affection that made Cait look away. She couldn't bear how the male looked at Alice with so much love in his eyes, not when Owen would never look at her that way again.

She had to get back to him.

She knew how to save his life now.

Cait looked at the two lion shifters and the males released her. She thanked Alice with another smile and then bolted for the alley that would lead her into the warren of streets.

Her heart lifted as she ran, tracking her scent back through the alleys.

She would save Owen.

She would save her mate.

That same heart missed a beat as she caught a familiar scent.

Dread twisted her stomach.

A sharp pain in the back of her left shoulder made her flinch and she staggered a few steps, turning her head to see what was wrong.

A dart with black and red feathers stuck out of her shoulder.

The world wobbled and swirled around her. Her knees turned to jelly, her right side slammed into a building, and she slid down it. Darkness bled across her vision but in the centre of it was a shadowy hazy figure.

One she recognised before slipping into a black abyss.

Marius.

CHAPTER 11

Fire burned in his bones, seared his mind, and licked across his skin. Owen shuddered and moaned as he kicked at the restrictive material covering him, trying to get it away so he could breathe again. He needed to breathe.

"Owen?" A soft female voice swirled around him.

Not the one he wanted to hear. Not Cait's sweet voice.

He groaned and fought the covers again. They were making him too hot. He needed air. Clean, cold air. He needed it to quench the fire blazing inside of him.

Something wet and cold spread across his forehead but it didn't cool him down. It didn't subdue the fire. That only grew hotter.

"Rest, Owen." Julianna's voice came again.

Rest? What had happened to him?

He remembered being with Cait, telling her things he shouldn't have, not only his secrets but his feelings too, baring all of himself to her. He remembered kissing her and then making love with her.

He remembered an incredible moment when he had felt connected to her, more than physically. The link had been emotional too and it had run deeper than blood in his body.

Blood.

He remembered something about blood.

"What happened?" he croaked and tried to open his eyes. His lashes stuck together, caked with gunk. What had been happening to him? He weakly lifted an arm that felt as if it was made of rubber. Julianna caught hold of it and settled it back on his chest.

She wiped a soft damp cloth across his eyes.

When she had finished, he opened them and looked up at her where she hovered above him, her dark eyebrows furrowed and concern shining in her rich brown eyes.

"You were bitten." Julianna sat back and reached off to her left, towards the small wooden side table beside his double bed.

Owen's eyes widened as he stared blankly at the ceiling, everything coming back to him now. He found the strength to shift his hand up to the left side of his throat and felt the marks there. It had felt incredible at the time and he hadn't given it a second thought, had been lost in the bliss of her bite and the mind-blowing release it had triggered in him.

Cait had bitten him. That single bite had infected him.

He was transitioning.

Julianna leaned back again, an ice-cold glass of water in her hand.

He stared at it, aching to take it from her and drink it down in one huge gulp. She caught hold of his arm and helped him to sit up on the bed, and brought the glass up to his lips. He drank it slowly, forcing himself to take it little by little rather than inhaling it. The cold slide of it down his throat was bliss that he didn't want to end. It spread through him, icy tendrils that quenched the fire.

He realised his cousin had given him more than water as the cooling sensation remained, helping to lower his temperature. She had put a spell in the water, one to help him, and he was grateful for it.

He needed one to restore his strength too. He didn't like feeling weak, his bones like rubber and muscles like water beneath his skin. He felt too close to death and it only increased his fear as he sat on the bed, listening hard for a sign of Cait in the other room.

Nothing.

He stared into Julianna's dark eyes. "Where's Cait?"

She looked away from him and his heart kicked in his chest, the fear of his weakness becoming a fear that something had happened to Cait. He loved Julianna, but he would never forgive her if she had driven Cait away from him in an attempt to protect him.

"What did you do to her?" Owen snapped.

Julianna's dark gaze darted to meet his. "Nothing. I came in soon after you passed out and she told me what had happened. I said I would look after you while she…"

"While she did what?" His heart began to pound and he looked beyond his cousin to the door that led into the living room.

She couldn't have.

"She went out to find a way of helping you," Julianna whispered.

She had.

He barked out a foul curse, lunged at his cousin and grabbed the front of her plain black dress, hauling her towards him. "She what?"

He didn't want to believe that Cait had gone out there alone, not when there were so many mercenaries on the prowl. Word of her would have spread through the town by now. One of those mercenaries might have contacted Marius.

"She's been gone a while."

Owen really hadn't wanted to hear those five words leaving his cousin's lips. Cold filled his veins and he could only stare at her, his heart labouring as he struggled to cope with the sudden deluge of fear and adrenaline.

"How long?" he snapped.

Julianna cast her gaze down at her knees and the cold inside Owen turned to ice.

"How long?" he barked, harder this time, narrowing his green eyes on her.

Julianna closed hers. "Over five hours."

His cousin suddenly lifted her head and clutched his arm, her eyes leaping between his and her eyebrows furrowing.

"I would have gone looking for her, but I couldn't leave you," she rushed out and her hand shook against his arm. "You were too sick... you are too sick."

"I'll be fine." Owen mustered his strength and shuffled to the edge of the bed beyond Julianna, where he had left his black jeans. "I have to find her. Something is wrong."

He bent forwards and his head spun as he grabbed his jeans from the floor. He struggled with them, making several attempts before he managed to get his feet into them. Sweat trickled down his bare back and down his cheeks from his brow. He breathed hard and forced himself to keep going as the room twisted around him.

"Owen," Julianna said and caught his shoulders as he began to fall backwards. She held him, her front against his back. "You're not strong enough."

He growled at her and shoved her away.

He wrestled with his jeans and got them up to his thighs, and crashed back onto the bed as he tugged them under the covers and over his hips. He managed two of the buttons, enough to keep them up, and rolled ungracefully onto his front. He grunted as he shoved his hands against the bed and his legs slid off the side of it. His bare feet landed on the wooden floor and he pushed onto them, rising unsteadily.

He stayed upright all of a second before his knees gave out, sending him crashing onto the floor. He spat out another curse.

He was stronger than this.

He knew about hellcats and he knew he stood a slim chance of surviving the transition, and an even slimmer chance if he overexerted himself, but he didn't care about himself.

He cared only about Cait.

He could find her.

She had bitten him.

There were countless spells he could use to track his own blood in her.

He *would* find her.

But first he had to do something about his weakness.

He crawled towards the door to the living room.

Julianna huffed and muttered something, and then she was beside him, grabbing his arms and helping him onto his feet. She slung his left arm around her shoulders and slowly walked with him into the cramped living room. He thanked her with a smile when she set him down on the wooden seat in front of his desk and then went to work.

He grabbed several jars of herbs from the shelves in front of him, instructing Julianna to take some others from the cupboard beside his desk as he worked to measure the right quantities.

When he mentioned nightshade, she stopped dead.

"It's too dangerous."

He grimaced and silently cursed her for knowing the spell, and then cursed himself when she looked at him and he realised that she had made an educated guess based on the ingredients rather than possessing the knowledge he had thought she had of the spell. His grimace had confirmed her suspicions.

She turned on him. "The spell might backfire. There's a reason it's a black art, one rarely made by modern witches. It's volatile and it's taboo, Owen, and you know it. I don't want to know how you know the spell… but I won't be a part of this. It might kill you."

He smiled solemnly. "I'm probably already done for… but what doesn't kill me makes me stronger, right?"

She looked as if she wanted to punch him, but instead she reached out and touched his cheek as she tried to smile. "Please, Owen."

He wished he could do as she was asking, but he couldn't. "I'll only take a small dose. Just enough to numb the pain."

He knew that the spell was dangerous, but it wasn't the first time he had used it. It was how he had gained a reputation as a silent killer, a sort of wraith.

A phantom born of shadows.

He would never tell Julianna that he had used this spell countless times. She would condemn him for it, the witch community would banish him for it, and he would probably deserve it. He was flirting with death each time he used it, but it had saved his life more times than he could count, turning jobs that would have killed him into ones he could survive and emerge from as the victor.

He was counting on it to save his life this time too, and not only because it would make it easier for him to slip into wherever Cait was being held and free her and fight the bastard who had taken her.

He took hold of Julianna's hand. "If I use this spell, I will be incorporeal. It might slow the transition because I won't have a physical form for it to affect. It's my one shot at helping Cait, and maybe saving myself in the process."

Julianna looked torn until he grunted as a fresh wave of fire seared his insides and he doubled over, clutching his stomach and shaking violently. Sweat rolled down his nose and dripped from the end, each tiny bead hitting his thigh and soaking into his black jeans as he rocked, fighting the pain and the nausea that came with it.

"Owen." Julianna poured another glass of water, crouched in front of him and helped him with it, slowly lifting it to his lips.

He managed to drink half of it before choking on it.

She patted him on his back, dislodging the water that had gone down the wrong tube, and then slowed to a gentle rubbing as he settled again. The fire abated but the iciness didn't flow through him this time, and he knew it wasn't because he had only managed to drink half of the concoction.

His condition was worsening.

"I don't have much time." Owen struggled to lift his head and look at his cousin.

Steely resolve filled her eyes and he stared at her, seeing another woman for a split-second. His mother. Julianna had her eyes and his mother had given him that same look a thousand times. It took him back to when he had been learning to wield magic and she had been pushing him not to give up, to keep fighting to master it, even when he had felt on the verge of collapse.

Fight filled him now as it had then, flooding his veins with the strength he needed, the resolve to keep battling and never give in.

He would save Cait.

Julianna rushed into action, gathering everything he had requested, including the jar of nightshade. She set it all out on the wooden table in front of him and stood beside him.

"Why do you need to help her? What's happened to her?"

Owen picked up a black upside-down-teardrop-shaped glass vial from the shelf at the back of his desk. It was beautiful yet grim, fitting for the potion he was about to make.

"Cait thought a male hellcat was after her to make a mate out of her." He stared at the vial, seeing his pale reflection in the curved glass. "I suspect that Marius has no intention of keeping her as a mate."

He lowered the vial and lifted his head, raising his eyes to his cousin's face. She stared at the vial he held, her gaze distant but filled with concern. She wasn't only worried about him. She was worried about Cait too.

"What will he do with her?" Julianna shifted her gaze down to meet his.

Owen closed his fist around the vial and frowned as a dark need filled him, a fierce desire to seek out Marius and destroy him for what he had planned for Cait.

"He's going to sell her on the black market."

CHAPTER 12

Cait slowly became aware of her surroundings. Quiet murmuring drifted around her, interspersed with some sort of chanting that was more distinct among the blend of sounds. She frowned and moaned as her head ached, her skull feeling as if someone had stuffed it full of cotton wool. The cold against her side sapped what little strength she had and she was vaguely aware that she had to move into another position, one that would keep her warmer.

A chill breeze blew across her naked flesh and she shivered and curled into a tighter ball.

It was no use. She couldn't remain where she was, even though she felt sure that if she tried to move, the entire world would begin spinning again and the ache in her head would grow worse.

She wriggled her arm free from beneath her and used it to lever herself up off the icy ground. The chanting nearby stopped and she felt eyes on her.

Cait drew in a deep breath and waited for her head to stop spinning violently before opening her eyes. They stung as the world struggled to come into focus for her. When it finally sharpened, she saw her worst nightmare.

She was in a cage. The black bars were as thick as her wrists, impossible for her to break if she had been at full strength, let alone hazy and weak as she was now.

Drugged.

She shuffled into a sitting position and rested her back against the bars on one side of her small four-foot wide cage. She mentally checked herself over and then fought her way through a visual check as her eyes switched between focused and hazy, the drug keeping her off balance. She frowned as she looked down and her chin hit cold metal.

Her eyes dropped to her chest and all of her hope died as she saw the thick steel collar around her neck.

It was loose now, but if she shifted into her more powerful form, it would be tight around her neck, choking her.

She needed to escape it.

She shoved at it, each weak attempt to push it up over her head stealing more of her strength, until all she could do was slump against the back of her cage and breathe, her hands limp in her lap.

What the hell had they given her?

She needed to get out of this place. She wasn't sure how long she had been unconscious, or where she was, but she had to break free of the cage and her collar. Owen needed her. His life depended on her returning to him and making him drink her blood. She couldn't be here.

She had to escape.

The thought of Owen suffering while she was trapped in the cage sent hot prickles dashing over her skin and she fumbled with the collar again, desperately tugging at it, refusing to let her weakness stop her this time.

When she couldn't get it off over her head, she focused, intent on shifting to see if her stronger form could help her break the cold steel.

Nothing happened.

She growled through her short fangs.

There was magic in the collar.

Cait used her brief burst of clarity to investigate her surroundings, because there was little point in escaping if she didn't have a route planned. She wasn't in any condition to fight. If she managed to break free of the cage, she needed to slip out quietly without drawing any attention.

She looked beyond her cage and realised that it was going to be impossible to avoid drawing attention to herself if she did escape.

She was in what appeared to be a sort of canyon. The black rock rose around her, cragged and sheer, leading her eye up to the dark sky above. Torches on thick wooden stands cast golden light across the walls and the oval space between them. There was only one exit if she couldn't clamber up the vertical walls, and it was at the far end of the oval. To reach it, she would have to navigate through a maze of cages of various sizes, all of them occupied by males and females. Mostly females.

She knew some of the species by smell. Close to her, in a small cage like her own, were two nude elf females clutching each other, their wrists bound by silver manacles and their violet eyes warily taking in their surroundings. If their restraints were anything like Cait's, they couldn't teleport to freedom and they were weakened by the magic in them.

Cait looked towards the source of the steady gaze she could feel pinned on her.

The solitary female sat in a black cage closest to Cait, directly opposite her. She was huddled into one corner, her knees held against her chest as she rocked, jangling the chain between her manacles. The female stared straight at Cait, unblinking. The dark crescents beneath her haunted eyes and the pallor of her skin warned Cait that this female had lived through a nightmare.

A nightmare Cait might be sharing soon.

The presence of the female told her one thing though.

They were in Hell.

Based on how the female appeared, covered in dirt and cuts, and bloodied and scarred around her wrists from the manacles, she had been captive for weeks or more.

If they were outside of Hell, the female would have been dead by now. She was a dragon.

Cait slowly shuffled towards the other side of the cage, closer to the female.

"Hello," she whispered, not wanting to draw any attention to them in case someone made a ruckus and guards came. She had to get information out of the female. "I'm Cait."

The dragon stared at her through dull eyes.

Cait tried a smile, hoping it might work. It didn't.

"What's your name?" she hissed in a low voice.

The dragon blinked. "Taryn."

Now she was getting somewhere. "What's happening?"

Taryn looked around and Cait noticed how unusual her eyes were as she turned her face towards the nearest torch. Her irises were rich purple around the outside, but in their centres around her pupils they were white. They matched her hair, which Cait could now see began as violet at the roots, but slowly faded to white at the tips.

"They will come soon," Taryn said, her tone distant but holding a haunted edge that chilled Cait to the bone. The dragon stared off into the distance towards the only exit. "Six times… each time it gets worse…"

Cait shuffled closer still, pressing against the bars as her head turned fuzzy again, derailing her thoughts. She waited for it to pass before speaking. "You've been through this six times?"

Taryn nodded and shifted her solemn gaze back to Cait. "I always fight the men who purchase me. I never let them near me… and then they grow angry and they bring me back and sell me… and replace me with someone compliant."

Cait wished she had the dragon's strength. Even bound as she was by steel and a spell, Taryn was probably stronger than Cait was without any drugs and magic inhibiting her.

"I want to be free," Taryn muttered and raised her strange eyes to the dark sky. "I want to fly. I need to fly."

She began rocking again and Cait reached through the bars of her cage to her, easily slipping her arm into Taryn's one. She strained, but couldn't quite reach the female dragon.

Taryn suddenly dropped her chin and stared at Cait through wide eyes. "I must escape."

Cait nodded. "I have no intention of letting these bastards sell me. I'll fight them. I will escape. Will you help me?"

81

Taryn began to nod and then shook her head. She lifted her hands, the chain between her silver manacles swaying from the action.

"I cannot shift."

Cait clutched the bars of her cage with both hands. "You are strong without your dragon side."

"I have to be free. I have to escape." Taryn's violet-to-white eyes turned wild and she crawled across the cage towards Cait and gripped the bars. "I must escape."

The female dragon nodded and looked to the sky again.

"We can escape," she whispered, her gaze distant and unfocused. "He is coming... I can feel it. Not for me... not yet... but when he comes... then we will be free."

"Who is coming?" Cait looked beyond Taryn to the only entrance, afraid that she meant that the guards and Marius were coming for them.

No one entered the oval area.

She shifted her focus back to Taryn, who continued to stare at the sky, a glassy quality to her eyes.

Some dragons had an incredible ability.

They could see the future.

Had Taryn seen their future?

"Who is coming, Taryn?" Cait grabbed her wrist and fought a bout of wooziness that came out of nowhere and made the world spin.

She swallowed hard and struggled through it, desperate to hear more about what Taryn had seen, needing to know who the male was because her heart was racing, her mind following it, rushing to a conclusion she feared would be wrong.

Owen couldn't be the male Taryn had seen.

Cait had to ask herself why he couldn't be the male. He was mortal, but he was a witch. A powerful one too. He could use one of the many portals that linked places in the mortal realm to places in Hell if he knew the right spell. He could track her with another spell. It had to be possible.

But it couldn't be Owen.

Owen was sick, dying because of her, weakened by the transition into a hellcat.

Her hope shattered and it felt as if her heart had shattered with it.

Had she not bitten him, Owen would have had the strength to cast the necessary spells to use a portal and even find her.

But she had bitten him. She had condemned him to death and now she faced life as a slave. She sagged against the bars and closed her eyes as that truth washed over her, carrying away the last fragments of her hope.

Taryn touched her hand. "He is coming."

Cait wished those words were about Owen, but she knew in her heart that they weren't. They were about another male, one Taryn had seen in a vision of the future. A male who would somehow set them free.

A tiny speck of hope clung to life in her aching heart and began to grow again.

Taryn had seen them escaping.

Cait couldn't give up now, not on securing her freedom and not on Owen. He was strong. He could survive long enough for her to find a portal and return to him. There would be a portal in the fae town. As soon as she landed there, she would save him.

Right now, she had to focus on saving herself.

A jeer went up a short distance away and Cait looked up at the top of the black cliffs off to her left. A glow lit the air there and she could smell people, a whole mass of them.

Taryn tensed. "It begins."

She looked beyond Taryn as a brawl broke out between a large blond male wearing dark clothing and a naked female. He held her by her long white hair, shoving her towards the exit.

Cait's eyes widened as two big dark-haired males dressed all in black pulled open two more cages and dragged their occupants out by their restraints—a male by his collar and a female by the chain between her wrists. These two didn't fight their guards. They walked with bowed heads. Cait wanted to shout at them to fight, but the look on Taryn's face warned her to keep quiet.

She could only sit in her cage as the others slowly emptied, listening to the jeering of the crowd and the bidding wars that erupted as each new piece of meat was auctioned. The oval area felt colder and colder with each pair of captives they pulled from it and Cait shrank further and further back into her cage, fear of what was to come battling against her sense of hope that Taryn was right and someone would free them.

She looked to the female dragon for reassurance.

Taryn smiled sadly. "It is time."

The next thing Cait knew, an immense dark-haired male dressed all in black was beside the cage, opening the lock on it. Every instinct she possessed told her to fight, but out of the corner of her eye, Taryn shook her head. Cait allowed the man to grab her arm and drag her from the cage. A second male pulled Taryn from her cage and marched her through the empty cages towards the exit.

The nude female dragon walked with her head held high, softly chanting, "He is coming."

Cait followed with her guard, breathing slowly to steady her nerves and keep her head from spinning. Whatever drug they had given her, the effect of it was beginning to fade. They had probably given her a dose that would last until the auction, intending for it to wear off before it was her turn to take to the stage so she would be nice and lucid for it.

She looked up as they passed through the narrow gap between the canyon walls and her guard dragged her left, down a natural corridor towards another open area. Steps formed the end of the corridor, leading up onto a high stage. The torches on it burned brightly, illuminating a sea of eager faces beyond. Her stomach turned and she had to fight for air as she drew closer to the stage, her panic rising and crushing her throat and lungs again.

Taryn walked steadily onwards and Cait tried to mimic her, not wanting to give the male waiting at the top of the steps the satisfaction of seeing her afraid.

Marius.

He loomed above her, clad all in black like the others, as she took the wooden steps up, her guard behind her now, shoving her in the back.

Marius's blue eyes narrowed as he smiled.

Cait wanted to claw it off his smug ugly face.

He grabbed hold of her collar when she was close enough and yanked her against him. He raised his hand, lifting her off her feet, and she flinched as the metal cut into her jaw and the back of her neck. She flinched again when Marius planted a wet kiss on her mouth and then growled and tried to bite the bastard's tongue off.

He tossed her onto the stage and clucked that tongue at her. "I was going to bid on you too."

She scowled at him and picked herself up, ignoring the hungry eyes that she could feel on her naked body as she turned to face Marius.

"I'm getting out of this collar, and when I do, I'm going to kill you," she snarled and tugged at the metal ring around her neck.

Marius chuckled and lifted his right hand.

Her guard pulled something from his belt and flicked his hand out. A long black stick extended in it and he brought it up in a fast arc, striking her hard across the side of her head. She cried out and staggered forwards from the force of the blow.

"Maybe I'll buy you just so I can break you." Marius smirked and she wanted to launch another verbal attack back at him, but the guard looked as if he was itching to deal another blow with his black baton.

She cursed him in her head and turned away from him, coming to face her audience for the first time.

She curled her lip at the slathering males from all different species, disgusted by how they raked their eyes over her and jostled for position closest to the stage. Some of the males and all of the females were already leaving with their purchases, ushering them towards the open end of the canyon.

There was a town in the distance. Pinpricks of yellow light in the darkness.

If she could make it there, she might find a portal.

She could guarantee that most of the people who had come to the auction hadn't been in the area. They must have travelled and the fastest way to travel in Hell were the portals.

"Shall we begin?" A deep male voice hollered and the crowd settled, their focus leaping to the owner of it.

The pale-haired male stood close to seven feet tall, his crimson eyes appraising her and then Taryn.

He was different to the guards and even Marius. More dangerous.

Deadly in fact.

The impeccable crisp black suit made him look the part of a charming and respectable businessman, and it could hide things about him that would make those less familiar with the creatures of Hell trust him, but she knew his kind.

She had met one once and that had been enough to imprint their scent on her instincts.

Instincts that had catalogued his entire kind as extremely dangerous and a species she didn't tangle with under any circumstances.

A fallen angel.

The seductive quirk to his sensual lips as his red gaze roamed back to her warned that he was on to her and knew she was staring at him for reasons other than his incredible looks. She dragged her gaze away before she gave him ideas about purchasing her for himself because she wouldn't last a second with a fallen angel.

They were sadistic and violent in everything they did.

Marius moved out of the corner of her vision, loping past the fallen angel to stand on the other side of the stage, together with other males who had no doubt supplied some of the people they had auctioned off tonight.

She bared her fangs at him.

The crowd jeered, evidently enjoying the show. Several shouted that they wanted to see the goods.

She didn't want to know what they meant by that. She was already naked. What more did they expect?

She tensed when the guard behind her snapped a thick chain onto her collar and whirled to face him, her eyes leaping from him to the length of steel links. They flowed across the stage and ended at a huge ring attached to a thick stone and steel post.

The male's fingers flexed around the grip of his black baton and he eyed her with sick excitement in his dark irises. He was going to enjoy whatever was about to happen and she wanted to claw his eyes out because of it.

Hush fell over the crowd and she snapped her head to her left when chanting filled the thick air.

A slender male dressed in a black suit who had been standing at the back of the stage beyond the fallen angel approached her, muttering something.

The sensation of restriction began to fade and strength flowed through her limbs.

He was unlocking the spell impregnated into the collar.

Dread rippled through her, cold and crippling as she realised what they were going to do.

The guard closed in behind her, raising his baton to strike.

Cait did the only thing she could in an attempt to escape the beating he wanted to deliver.

She shifted.

Black fur swept over her skin as her limbs twisted, bones snapping out of place and reforming in the blink of an eye. She growled through her clenched fangs and fell onto her paws as her twin tails snaked from the base of her spine, her face changed and her ears moved upwards, becoming rounded. She snarled and blue fire leaped from between her teeth.

The crowd jeered again.

The guard hit her with the baton.

Cait turned on him and hissed when he grabbed the length of chain attached to her tight collar and yanked on it, choking her. She pulled away from him, trying to avoid being struck again, but he tugged her closer, too strong for her to resist. She growled as she realised that the male witch had only lifted the spell enough for her to regain a small fraction of her strength, all that she needed to shift into her hellcat form.

The guard brought the baton down hard again, striking her hindquarters. She snarled, baring her fangs at him. The blue glow emanating from her grew stronger as her anger rose, the hunger for violence within her rising with it, causing the fire that constantly swept across the tips of her tails to engulf their entire lengths and burst from her paws too.

Something inside her snapped when Taryn cried out and she whipped her head around.

The other guard held Taryn by her long purple-to-white hair while the fallen angel ran his hands down her naked body, pressing short claws into her flesh and leaving red score marks in their wake.

"This one would be well worth the pain of breaking her," the fallen angel said with a wicked smile and a dark sadistic glint in his red eyes.

Several males in the audience began shouting numbers.

Cait roared and launched herself at the fallen angel. She sailed through the air, intent on knocking the disgusting male away from Taryn and helping her. The chain attached to her collar jerked tight and yanked on the metal ring that bit into her throat, stopping her in mid-air. She dropped and landed hard on the stage.

The fallen angel turned his cruel smile on her.

"No need to rush... I shall appraise you next. *Thoroughly.*"

Cait hunkered down as he turned towards her, growling at him and flicking her twin tails side to side. The darkness around him seemed to grow with each slow step towards her that he took, his red eyes beginning to glow in the low light.

Fear beat through her, too strong for her to master.

The tips of his emerging fangs showed between his lips as his smile widened.

His claws grew longer.

Cait lost her fight against her urge to cower.

"He comes," Taryn murmured.

The fallen angel's smile faded.

Cold blasted through the arena and Cait shuddered as it sucked the heat from her sleek body.

Black shadows swept in and swirled around, blanketing everything.

Screams pierced the darkness.

CHAPTER 13

Owen was pushing his luck, the shadow spell taking its toll on his body every time he renewed it, but he had a feeling that it had been worth the strange sensation that he was losing himself. It had taken him two days of tracking his own blood, but he had finally found what he had been looking for.

The people coming and going through the seedy medieval-looking town in the free realm of Hell spoke of an auction, unaware of him as he lurked in the shadows, one with them. Unless he chose to make his presence known, the spell kept him cloaked and incorporeal.

A wraith.

He looked down the main thoroughfare of the town, off to his right, towards endless black where only a single distant glow broke the darkness.

Many of the unsavoury males were heading in that direction, their excited murmurs about what goods they intended to purchase sickening him and making him want to kill them all and do the world a favour. He couldn't expend that much power though. He would need all that he had left if he was going to save Cait.

Owen moved towards the glow, crossing the uneven black land at speed, floating like a phantom above it.

A canyon loomed ahead, formed of cragged obsidian rock. He rose up one of the steep inclines to the plateau at the top and drifted across it, following the sound of cheering.

When the large open area amidst the black rock came into view, Owen stopped dead and scowled down at the people crammed into the makeshift arena. At the far end across from him stood a stage and two immense dark-haired males dressed in black were parading a naked male and female across it, using batons to keep them in line. Another male, this one blond and dressed in a tailored dark suit, played the role of auctioneer, whipping the crowd into a buying frenzy.

Owen used his time wisely as he waited for Cait to appear, scanning the crowd and seeking out any dangerous opponents he needed to be aware of before he launched an attack. Most of the crowd weren't a threat to him. They were weaker species, which left Owen despising them even more. They purchased their slaves to give them a sick sense of power.

The smartly dressed male on the stage didn't need to sink to such low levels to feel powerful. He possessed strength, a deadly and dangerous edge to his aura, one that left Owen determined to avoid a direct confrontation with him.

He had met a fallen angel once.

It was the only job he had failed.

Owen was no match for the strength of the male, not even on his best day. Definitely not when he was liable to collapse into a writhing heap of agony the second he lifted his shadow spell.

The fallen angel could finish him with a single blow.

He spotted Marius moving to the canyon corridor that led off the back of the stage and clenched his fists at his sides, filled with an overwhelming need to fly down and tear the male to pieces for taking Cait from him.

The current auction ended and a nude female with dark-to-light hair came onto the stage, escorted by one of the guards.

Owen's fury faded as he saw Cait behind her.

His beautiful Cait.

They had put a collar on her, just as she had feared, and he wanted to rip it off her and set her free.

He wanted to gather her into his arms and hold her, because there was fear in her eyes as she looked at Marius and then the crowd. He would take that fear away for her.

He moved around the edge of the canyon, drawing closer to her, waiting for the right moment to strike and barely holding himself back as Marius dared to plant a kiss on Cait. Owen plotted Marius's death in his head as Cait broke free and turned on the hellcat male.

The crowd jeered and shouted demands, and Cait's guard attached a chain to her collar, tying her to a thick post. Owen readied his weapon again as another male in a dark suit approached Cait, a sense of power flowing from him.

Magic.

Owen knew that spell. They were restraining Cait by using it on her collar and he suspected the same spell was in the other female's shackles.

Before the guard could strike Cait, she had shifted, becoming a beautiful sleek black cat with twin tails that flickered with blue fire.

Owen began to chant beneath his breath as he prepared himself, sensing that everything was about to take a turn for the worse and his time to act was coming.

The fallen angel turned towards Cait as she tried to launch herself at him and failed. The male stalked towards her, vicious intent on his face, and she cowered, going down on her belly and backing away from him. He meant to hurt her. Never.

Owen would never let the male lay a finger on Cait.

A sudden outbreak in fighting in the middle of the crowd snapped Owen's attention to that spot. Several males dressed in tight black armour appeared one after the other, led by one with wild blue-black hair and a long obsidian spear.

Elves.

Owen saw his chance and took it.

He unleashed the spell he had been chanting and it swept across the canyon, sucking all of the heat from the air as the shadows swirled and blanketed the area, plunging it into darkness.

He could see though.

The elves continued their fight, decimating the crowd as they pushed through it, evidently using their heightened senses to guide them towards whatever they had come for.

On the stage, the other female dropped to her knees, breaking free of the guard who held her hair. She roared and sprang, launching herself at the fallen angel's back where he stood in the middle of the stage, looking around him, his red eyes glowing brightly.

Owen leaped from the edge of the canyon and landed silently on the ground below the cragged black wall of rock. He couldn't fight as he was. The spell made it impossible and the moment he lifted it to attack, the shadows would lift too, dissipating in a heartbeat.

He swept through the crowd as they blindly ran, bumping into each other. Some made the unfortunate mistake of ending up in the path of the elves as they hacked their way through the darkness, cutting down any who dared to get in their way.

Owen lifted the spell as he kicked off, leaping onto the black stage.

The light from the torches instantly flickered into life, driving the shadows back and revealing the battle that had broken out. The cold lingered in the air though, cool against his bare chest, fighting the heat that began to rise inside him again as his body became solid once more.

The fallen angel bared his fangs on a hiss, huge black wings burst from his back and he kicked upwards, launching into the air. Fleeing. Owen didn't care. He wasn't here to throw what remained of his life away on fighting a fallen angel.

He was here to save Cait and make Marius pay.

His narrowed eyes slid towards Marius as he fled the stage and he threw his right hand towards him, releasing a twisting black and red orb. The spell struck the male in the back, sending him flying forwards down the steps into the canyon.

No escape for the bastard now.

Owen shifted his focus to Cait, chanting the spell that would reverse the one restraining her as he ran towards her. The other female landed hard where the fallen angel had been and growled through sharp teeth, her strange eyes flashing dangerously as she pinned them on him. She thought he was a threat.

Cait sniffed, her nose lifted high in the air, and then lowered her head and snarled at the female, black fur sticking up along her spine. She had scented him. He threw his hand towards the chain that held her and it shattered, the links breaking apart and flying in all directions.

The female immediately backed off and turned her rage on those who were a threat to them.

Cait looked back at him, her blue eyes bright in the low light. She changed back, writhing and growling as her body transformed and her black fur disappeared, leaving pink skin behind. He wanted to cover her with something, the thought of all the males in the area seeing her naked turning his blood to fire, but he couldn't spare the magic or his strength.

She didn't seem to care as she ran at him, hurled her arms around his neck, and kissed him hard.

Owen gathered her against him, his heart pounding and relief coursing through him as he felt her in his arms, her naked chest pressing against his bare one. Reality sank in swiftly to chase all of his fears away. She was safe now. All he had to do was get her out of this place and deal with the male who had put her here, and then he was done and he could rest.

The other female launched a brutal attack on one of the guards, raining blows down on him and managing to get his baton. She smacked the male across the head with it and he grunted and hit the deck, landing in a slump on the wooden boards.

Owen pressed his hand to Cait's collar. It snapped open in response to his spell and he smiled as she tore it off her. She smiled back at him and wobbled in his vision.

"Not now," he muttered and pressed his hand to his head, screwing his eyes shut as he fought the wave of nausea that ripped through him.

His knees buckled, the force of them hitting the stage sending a numbing jolt up his spine.

"Owen," Cait shouted, dropped to her knees beside him and grabbed his shoulders. "Owen?"

He sucked down a sharp breath into his burning lungs and nodded, trying to let her know that he would be alright. For now at least. He wasn't sure how much longer he had and he still needed to get Cait away from this place.

His hands shook as he fumbled for the remaining vial of the spell Julianna had made for him. He almost had it free of the pouch on the belt of his black jeans when another wave of dizziness crashed over him. Cait clutched him with one hand, keeping him steady, and reached for the pouch with the other.

"Clear vial." He managed to squeeze those words out, afraid she would give him the black one instead. He couldn't risk becoming a shadow again. He might not have the strength to make himself corporeal again.

She nodded and pulled the slender glass vial out, popped the cap off and brought it up to his lips. She poured it into his mouth. It instantly cooled the burning in his throat and his lungs as it went down and he sighed as it spread through him, stealing away his pain and the dizziness, leaving him able to fight again.

"We have to get out of here," he said and stumbled onto his feet.

Cait hesitated. "I have to help Taryn."

She looked behind her at the female where she was fighting the other guard and losing. The manacles were stealing her strength and inhibiting her. He nodded and Cait rushed to her aid, taking on the guard for her. The other men who had been on the stage had scattered, but Owen knew one of them hadn't gone far.

Marius.

The bastard had ducked into the canyon beyond the stage but he wouldn't get away. The spell Owen had hit him with was a tracker. No matter where the male hellcat went, Owen could find him now. He would pay for what he had done to Cait.

Owen muttered the spell that would lift the one on Taryn's manacles as he stumbled towards her. Cait had the baton and seemed quite taken with the black weapon as she fought the guard, landing hard blows on his arms and his legs before leaping back to a safe distance as the male retaliated.

When Owen was close enough to Taryn and had finished the incantation, he stared at her manacles around her wrists and threw his hand forwards to unleash the spell. The restraints snapped open and fell from her arms, and she looked across at him, a flicker of gratitude in her violet-to-white eyes. What species was she?

She leaped into the fray before he could ask, helping Cait with the guard and taking him down with a single devastating blow.

Whatever she was, she was incredibly powerful.

The elves closed in on the stage, cutting through the remains of the crowd below him, and Owen spotted what they were after. Two elf females were huddled together near the corner of it ahead of him, wedged against the front of the stage and the canyon wall. Three males stood in front of them but they would be no match for the seven elf warriors coming at them.

A sensation went through Owen and he bit out a curse.

He turned back towards Cait and Taryn. "Marius is on the move."

Cait glanced at him and then looked at Taryn. "Come with us."

Owen looked back at the elves as they dealt with the last of the three men and carefully took the two female elves into their custody. He wished he could help them with their manacles, but he needed every last drop of his magic for the fight against Marius.

"Thank you, but I have to go," Taryn said. "I have to fly."

The elf warrior with the spear spun on his heel to face Taryn, his violet eyes wide. Owen looked to the female too. She was looking at the elf.

A heartbeat of time passed, a silent second in which the two merely stared at each other, and then the male lifted his hand and touched the left side of his neck, resting his fingers on the scales of his black armour.

Taryn turned away and Owen couldn't believe his eyes as she transformed right in front of him, becoming an enormous dragon with violet scales that turned white down her throat and under her belly. White leathery membrane stretched as she beat her huge wings and threw her head back, her curved white horns almost touching her neck as she roared, the sound deafening as it echoed around the canyon.

"Wait!" The elf male launched onto the stage in a single leap, landing at her side.

She snarled through fangs each the length of Owen's arms and swept her gigantic left paw down in a devastating arc, catching the elf male and sending him flying into a wall of black rock across the canyon.

"Commander Bleu," one of the other elves called after him and teleported, appearing beside the fallen male.

The one called Bleu picked himself up, shook himself and then growled as Taryn took flight, the wind from each hard beat of her wings battering Owen and Cait. Bleu teleported and appeared on the stage in front of Owen, his gaze on the beautiful dragon as it disappeared into the gloom. He bit out something harsh sounding in a strange tongue, tossed Owen a black scowl, and turned on his heel, storming across the stage towards the group of elves that waited for him with the two females.

"He is coming... I thought Taryn meant you," Cait murmured and looked up into Owen's eyes as she approached him, concern and warmth flooding her blue irises. "But she meant him... the elf."

"They know each other?" Owen said and Cait shrugged, drawing his attention back to the fact that she was naked.

He slowly moved towards the unconscious guards and set about pulling the black t-shirt off one of them for her. Sweat broke out across his brow and he wavered, his strength threatening to leave him again as his fever returned fiercer than ever.

"Owen." Cait caught him around the waist when his knees weakened and held him up. He thanked her with a small smile and hated how concerned she looked, the fear back in her eyes again. Fear for him this time.

"I'm okay." He hated himself for lying to her too. Especially when she responded by giving him a look filled with sorrow, as if he was already dead. "I told you once I was made of sterner stuff than you think."

He held the t-shirt out to her and fought the wave of dizziness, refusing to let it send him swaying on his feet when he was trying to reassure her.

"I know. I'm sorry about what I did... if I—"

He cut her off by pressing his finger against her lips. "We can talk about it later."

He offered the t-shirt again and she took it this time, slipping it on over her head. It dwarfed her, but at least that meant it covered all the distracting parts of her, allowing him to focus again.

"Ready?" he said and she nodded. He took hold of her hand, clutching it in his, and looked down at her, absorbing her beauty and the affection that shone in her blue eyes as she stared at him, stealing every last drop of her attention because it gave him strength when he had none left. Only his feelings for her, his need to protect her and ensure she would be safe, were keeping him going now. "Good, then let's go... because I have a job to do."

A job he finally felt would be the end of him.

For the first time in his life, he feared death.

He feared it because he didn't want to leave Cait behind.

He didn't want to lose her just as he had found her.

He wanted to be with her.

He wanted to live with her.

The woman he had fallen in love with.

CHAPTER 14

Cait caught Owen as he almost fell down the steps that led into the canyon, grabbing his left arm and holding him upright. He shot his right hand out, pressing it into the black rock wall, and breathed hard. Beads of sweat dotted his brow and he closed his eyes, the muscle of his jaw popping as he clenched his teeth.

He was in a worse condition than he had let on and she cursed him for trying to hide how dire his situation was from her.

"I have a cure," she said and slung his arm around her, helping him down the rest of the wooden steps.

He grunted in response.

"I have to get you somewhere and give you my blood." She didn't want to mention what came after that stage. He didn't need to know that she would have to hurt him, not when he was already weak and probably feeling vulnerable.

Owen shook his head. "Marius."

"I know we have to find him… but can't it wait?" She looked across at Owen as she guided him along the corridor, supporting his weight. He was burning up against her, his bare torso slick with sweat, and she could feel him shaking.

Time was running out for him. It was a miracle he had survived this long. He wouldn't last much longer though.

Owen managed to shake his head again.

"Leave you vulnerable," he gritted out and she realised that was the reason why he didn't want her to give him her blood.

He was worried about her.

She wanted to hit him for being more worried about her than he was about himself, treating himself as unimportant. He was important.

He was important to her.

"I don't care," she bit out and weathered his scowl as he turned to face her. "I only care about you, Owen."

His green eyes softened and he slowly lifted his right hand and settled it against her cheek. "Cait."

When he leaned more heavily on her, his face paling further, she made the decision for him. She set him down on the floor of the canyon and leaned him against the wall. It didn't matter if she left herself vulnerable by giving Owen her blood. All that mattered was ensuring he would survive.

She couldn't lose him.

She looked him in the eye and lifted her right wrist to her mouth, her fangs elongating in preparation to sink into her flesh and draw her blood for him.

A blow came out of nowhere, connecting hard with the left side of her head and knocking her down into the black dirt.

A bright flash of purple light chased back the darkness as Owen threw his hand to his right, towards the area where she had been held in a cage. The blast of magic struck Marius directly in his chest, hurling him through the air.

"Cait." Owen tried to reach for her and wavered, slumping forwards.

She shoved herself onto her knees again, caught his arms and righted him. Her eyes darted between his and she growled when she saw how dull they were and felt him trembling beneath her hands.

"I've got this," she whispered and smoothed her fingers across his brow, brushing the sweat-soaked strands of his dark hair from it as she smiled at him. She lowered her head and swept a kiss across his lips, lingering for a moment to savour the intimate caress and his tender response. "Just wait here. I'll be right back."

She didn't wait for him to nod or give her any indication he would do as she had asked. She launched to her feet and ran at Marius where he was picking himself up off the ground near the entrance to the area where they had kept her in a cage.

He was going to pay in blood for that.

Marius spotted her and scrambled across the dusty ground, disappearing down the corridor to her right, heading into the oval area beyond. She growled and sprinted after him, afraid of leaving Owen behind but unwilling to let Marius escape. The quicker she dealt with him, the sooner she could return to Owen. She needed to end this in order to save Owen, because Marius would keep trying to attack her whenever she let her guard down to give Owen her blood.

Her senses sparked in an alert and she dropped, hurling herself feet first across the ground, sliding into the oval area and under the blade Marius had swung at her.

She dug her heels into the ground to stop herself from sliding and rolled onto her front. She kicked off and sprang at Marius, seizing hold of his arm before he could move to block her attack. He howled in agony as she sank her teeth into his bare arm and tore at his flesh, ripping deep grooves in it with her fangs. The sharp coppery tang of his blood filled the air and he dropped the weapon as he turned on her, slamming his left fist into her chest to knock her back.

Cait released him and flipped backwards, landing on her feet a short distance away. Marius gave chase, the weapon forgotten as he came at her hard and fast, his eyes flashing bright blue. He bared his fangs on a snarl and black fur rippled over his exposed skin.

She beat him to the shift, tearing her t-shirt off and transforming as quickly as she could manage, snarling as pain tore through her as her limbs twisted and altered and black fur swept over her body. She twitched her twin tails and blue fire swept down them, covering their entire lengths, and burst from beneath her paws.

Marius completed his shift, becoming a larger version of herself, a sleek black beast with blue fire flickering along his tails and from between his fangs. His eyes glowed brightly and fire blazed around his paws as he growled and launched himself at her.

Cait rolled to evade him and swiped at his hindquarters with her claws. She missed.

Marius skidded on the sandy ground and pounded towards her, the blue fire beginning to twine up his legs as he called on more of his strength. She sprang into the air as he reached her, leaping high over him and twisting over to ensure she landed on her paws. Marius slammed into her side the second she made contact with the ground, knocking her down.

He landed on top of her, his fangs flashing in the low light as he struck at her throat. Cait rolled onto her back and kicked hard, scratching his belly with her claws. He grunted and hissed and raked his claws down her right cheek.

Cait snarled and smacked him hard, slamming her left front paw into his jaw at the same time as she kicked him with her back legs, sending him up into the air. She rolled away from beneath him and came up onto her paws.

Blue fire twisted around her legs and burned brighter, growing as her anger began to consume and control her, birthing a need for violence and bloodshed.

The male hellcat bared his fangs at her and his fire engulfed his body. Cait growled and allowed hers to do the same, the heat of it flickering and licking across her fur stoking her fury as she stared him down, daring him to make the first move.

The walls of the canyon glowed blue from their fire as Marius stared right back at her, his bright cerulean eyes becoming almost white as he stalked towards her, his shoulders shifting beneath his black fur with each measured step.

He threw his head side to side and growled just before he ran at her.

Cait readied herself to leap, her muscles twitching beneath her fur, and launched into the air as he closed in on her. He leaped too, colliding with her in mid-air and taking her down onto the dirt. She struggled beneath him, snarling and growling, trying to kick him off her.

He had read her body and had known what she had intended to do. She had left herself wide open to attack and he had seized the opportunity she had given him.

His weight pressed down on her and she wasn't strong enough to break free from underneath him this time.

She roared in agony as his head came down, his jaws clamping around her throat, fangs pressing into her flesh. Pain blazed through her, white-hot and burning her to ashes inside as she struggled beneath him, clawing and kicking him, trying to break free before he strangled her. She couldn't lose. Owen was waiting for her.

His life depended on her.

She hissed and raked her claws over Marius's head, her blue flames clashing with his, sparking whenever they touched.

Marius bit down harder and Cait fought for air, her vision beginning to swim as he cut off her supply and the pain grew more intense, too much for her to bear.

She whimpered, weakly fighting against Marius, her paws too heavy to lift as he starved her body of oxygen.

She stared at the dark sky and prayed to her gods, wishing she could have seen Owen one last time and asking them to bring them together in the afterlife to give her the forever she had begun to want with him.

A bright blue blast zipped across the darkness from her right like lightning, struck Marius and sent the male hellcat flying through the air as he growled in pain.

Cait breathed hard, wheezing as air suddenly rushed into her burning lungs, and her eyes watered as her head fell to her right, towards the source of the blast that had saved her.

Owen lay on his front on the black ground in the entrance to the oval area, his right hand still outstretched in front of him, tiny blue sparks leaping between his fingers.

She rolled over and grunted as she shifted back as quickly as she could manage while she was still struggling to overcome the effects of Marius's attack on her. When she had transformed, she shoved onto her feet and staggered towards Owen. She ran her gaze over him, reassuring herself that he was unharmed, and grabbed the sword from the dirt beside him.

She had to finish this.

She wasn't strong enough to take Marius out in her cat form.

But she could cut the bastard's head off in her normal form.

Owen muttered something beneath his breath and closed his eyes, stretching his right hand out towards the other end of the oval. The metal cages that filled that end of it began to shudder and lift off the ground.

Blue fire erupted in the darkness again as Marius found his feet and the flames swept back over his entire body, covering him from his nose to the tips of his tails.

Cait breathed hard and readied her blade, preparing herself to take whatever chance Owen was working to give to her.

A green glow lit Owen's hand and tiny orbs began to race around it, zipping between his fingers and twisting around his palm. The black metal cages shot into the air and Marius turned on them with a snarl and kicked off. Too late. The first cage hit the dirt in the direction he had been about to run, forcing him to bank right. A second cage dropped there, almost hitting him. Marius growled and banked left this time, but a third cage blocked his way. He turned and ran towards Cait and she realised what Owen was doing.

He wasn't trying to hit Marius.

He was driving Marius into her path.

She launched herself forwards, gripping the blade with both hands, holding it down at her right side.

Owen dropped three more cages as Marius attempted to run at her, breaking his stride and forcing him to keep twisting and turning, skidding left and right on the black dusty ground. There were only two more cages left. Cait had to position herself to make them count. She skidded behind one of the cages that had already fallen and stayed low, out of sight of Marius.

He began to run at Owen instead and Owen dropped the last two cages on either side of Marius, forcing him to stay on a collision course with him.

The moment Marius had passed her, Cait sprang from her hiding place, launched up onto the top of one of the last cages Owen had dropped and kicked off from it, propelling herself through the air. She tucked her right knee against her stomach and left her other leg trailing behind her as she brought her sword back over her head. She set her sights on Marius as he closed in on Owen, forcing herself to focus on the male hellcat rather than her mate, knowing that if she looked at Owen, it would distract her.

Because he had passed out.

She began to descend towards Marius. He bared his fangs and dipped low, preparing himself to leap on Owen.

Cait didn't give him the chance.

The moment he kicked off with his back legs, she brought her sword down in a swift and deadly arc, putting all of her strength into the single blow to his neck. The blade cleaved straight through his spine, the bone grating against the metal and turning her stomach, and sliced clean through his flesh, severing his head.

His body instantly slumped and skidded across the ground. His head rolled across it, the fire in his blue eyes spluttering out. It came to a halt near Owen.

Cait landed silently on the ground, took two swift strides towards Owen, dropping the sword along the way, and kicked the head away from him. It rolled into the darkness.

She didn't take a moment to celebrate defeating Marius because it didn't matter to her, not when Owen was lying unconscious on the ground in front of her, his life in grave danger.

She dropped to her knees beside him, rolled him onto his back so he lay against her thighs, and brought her left wrist up to her lips. She sank her fangs into it and gave a deep pull on her own blood to get it flowing. The coppery liquid flooded her mouth and she filled it before pulling her wrist away, bending over Owen, and placing her mouth on his. She coaxed his jaw open with her left hand and let her blood flow from her mouth and into his in a kiss that she hoped would be enough to give them a shot at forever.

He was still as her blood flowed into him and she rubbed his throat, convincing him to swallow it. His throat worked beneath her fingers and he moaned as he took her blood into his body. She drew back and stared down at him, brushing his tangled dark hair from his brow as she waited for him to come around. He was burning up again, sweat making his ashen skin slick beneath her fingers.

"Owen," she murmured and lowered her left wrist to his mouth. "Drink for me now, Owen. Take what you need."

His lips parted and she placed her wrist over them, her eyes locked on his face as he began to drink from her vein. He paled further and shuddered. His hands came up, trying to shove her wrist away from his mouth, and she sensed his panic. She wrapped her right arm around him and clutched him to restrain him as she forced her left wrist against his lips.

"You need it, Owen... don't fight it. I'm right here. I'm with you. Don't you want to be with me too?" She bit back her tears as they burned her eyes and held on to him, hoping he knew she was the one with him and that he was safe. "Take my blood, Owen... it will make this nightmare end for both of us."

He began drinking again, stronger this time, and his shivering started to subside but more sweat broke out across his brow and his bare chest, turning his skin shiny in the light from the torches.

When her head turned and weakness swept through her, she reluctantly pulled her wrist away from his bloodied lips, hoping that she had given him enough.

She looked down at him before lowering her head and pressing a kiss to his lips. Her stomach turned, flipping over and over as she thought about what she had to do next.

She had to face the worst part.

She needed to make him shift.

"I'm sorry," she whispered, her lips brushing his damp forehead as she fought for the strength to do what she had to do in order to save him.

She drew back and found him looking at her, his green eyes dull but focused on her. She smiled and stroked his hair, wishing with all of her aching heart that there was another way, because she had already put him through too much pain and suffering.

"I don't want to do this but I have to… you need to understand that. I don't have a choice." Her eyebrows furrowed as she looked down at him and concern grew in his green eyes as they moved between hers.

They lost their focus and began to slip shut but he managed to open them again. She could feel the effort it had taken for him to do that and it was clear to her that he was losing his fight. Her blood had given him back a fraction of his strength, but it was fading fast as his body consumed it.

She had to do it now, or she was going to lose him forever.

Cait gently laid him down on the black ground.

"I have to make you shift." She forced herself to hold his dull gaze as it widened, a flicker of understanding sparking in it.

He knew what she had to do.

She pulled down a deep breath, expelled all of her fear and pain on a sharp exhale, and rose onto her feet. She picked up the sword she had discarded and Owen eyed it, no fear in his green gaze. Only understanding.

"It will hurt… and I'm sorry." Cait moved to stand over him, her hand shaking against the hilt of the silver blade.

Owen croaked, "Do it."

His sensual bloodied lips tilted into a smile and it touched her, filling her with warmth, because she knew it was meant to comfort her and give her strength.

She nodded and poised the point of the blade above his left shoulder, a place where it would hurt him enough to force him to shift but wouldn't be a dangerous wound.

She took one last look into his eyes, seeing the conviction in them, before looking away, unable to bring herself to watch as she hurt the man that she had fallen in love with. Tears rolled down her cheeks as she drove the blade down into his shoulder and she closed her eyes as his agonised cry shattered the still air.

Cait clenched her jaw and pushed deeper.

Owen's cry became a fierce growl.

He lashed out, knocking the blade away from him and out of her grip. It tumbled across the black ground and her gaze whipped from it to Owen as he roared. He arched off the ground, every muscle on his torso and arms straining as he bellowed at the sky, and then flipped onto his side and curled up into a ball, shaking all over.

She backed off a step, giving him room as he snarled and kicked out, pain written across every line of his face and beating within her too. He struck at the ground, slamming his fists against it one moment and clawing at it with his fingertips the next. His nails grew darker, turning black.

Cait's heart almost stopped.

He was shifting.

He rolled onto his front, shoved onto his hands and knees and arched his back towards the sky as he growled, his head hanging between his arms. Patchy fur rippled across his bare skin, as black as midnight.

"Owen," she whispered and edged closer. "You can do this, Owen... I know you can. You're strong."

He lifted his head and snarled at her, his green eyes gaining a blue shimmer as he bared his blunt teeth. She backed off again and her heart went out to him when he slammed his hands against the dirt and screamed, his pain tearing at her. Shifting was painful enough for her, and she was used to it. She couldn't imagine what it was like for him.

His elbows gave out and he hit the dirt face-first, going terribly still as his breathing turned shallow and unsteady.

No.

Cait was on her knees in a heartbeat, gathering him to her, pulling him across her thighs. His head lolled and she fought the tears that sprang into her eyes, blinding her. She dashed them away and pressed her left wrist back against his mouth. He didn't move.

"Come on, Owen. Prove to me that you're strong." She rubbed her wrist across his mouth.

He snarled and bit down on it, and she cried out as pain tore up her arm.

He sucked hard, sending her head spinning, and swallowed the blood he had taken. The moment he swallowed, he released her wrist and yelled at the top of his lungs as the bones in his hands twisted and bent out of shape, his claws growing longer. His heart laboured in her ears as he rolled off her and shoved her away, sending her falling backwards.

He crawled away from her, breathing hard and snarling.

Her heart lurched as he slumped again.

Fear flooded her.

He wasn't going to make it.

The process of the transition and the pain of trying to change was stealing too much of what little strength he had left. She had to do something to help him or the exertion was going to kill him.

Deep in her heart, within her soul, her most primal instincts burst into life and ignited a spark of hope.

Cait gave in to the desire that swept through her, a compulsion to change, both to reassure him with her presence as another hellcat and to show him how it was done.

She crawled to him and he looked at her, his green-to-blue eyes filled with pain, agony that made her want to look away because she had caused it. She refused to give in to that need, shunning that weaker part of herself and focusing on the stronger part.

The part that loved this man and was going to save him.

The moment she was sure he was paying attention to her, she began to shift, changing her paws first. Her fingers bent as his had, distorting into a different form beneath her skin, shrinking as her palm grew wider and her hand grew thicker. The pain of changing slowly had her own heart labouring but Owen needed her to do this for him.

His eyes studied everything she did and then her hope soared as his hands changed too, forming two large paws.

Confident that he could follow her instructions, she looked back and changed her hind legs, drawing his attention to them. He mimicked her, growling as his bones snapped out of place, shrinking or growing, altering to fit his new form. When they had shifted, he kicked his jeans away, struggling out of them.

She changed her arms next, completing them, and then focused on her body. Owen followed every change that she made, his body altering to match hers, his heart growing stronger as he progressed further into his shift.

His twin tails whipped out from the base of his spine before she had started to form hers and black fur swept over him, covering him from head to toe.

Cait concentrated on changing her head, allowing her ears to shift upwards and become rounded, and her cheeks to puff up around her flattening nose, and her teeth to elongate.

She finished her shift and waited for Owen to catch up. He struggled and she licked his neck, encouraging him and showing him that she was with him. He only had to change one more thing and he was done. He would have completed his first shift.

She rubbed her cheek against him and purred deep in her throat.

He snarled, lowered his head and scrubbed his paws over his face as he changed it. His eyes turned completely blue as they grew larger and his nose flattened and grew broader. Huge teeth flashed between his jaws as he opened them. His ears were the last thing to change, morphing into a new rounded shape as they settled into place at the top of his head.

He collapsed beside her, breathing hard, larger than she was in her cat form and infinitely more beautiful.

Tiny blue flames appeared around his teeth as he breathed, shifting with each inhale and exhale. He was weak right now, his flames small because of it, but they would grow in strength as he did.

Cait nursed him, licking his damp fur and cleaning the dirt off it, making it glossy as he lay beside her, slowly regaining his strength. She moved around to his other side when she had finished cleaning his entire right one, and started by licking his ear.

He lifted his head and rubbed his cheek across her nose.

Relief coursed through her, sweet and strong, stealing away the last of her strength as she realised that he was finally safe.

He had survived.

She nudged him to see whether he would move and he lumbered onto his paws, staggering for a few steps before he found his balance. He looked across at her, his bright blue eyes gaining focus, and she picked up her discarded t-shirt and his jeans in her mouth and began walking towards the exit into the canyon, slowly so she didn't lose him.

He followed and she waited for him at the corridor. When he had caught up with her, she rubbed him again, brushing her cheek across his, and he made a low coughing noise in his throat. She set the clothes down and chuffed back at him, letting him know that she was with him and offering him the comfort he had instinctively sought.

She encouraged him each step of the way as they walked, seeking a place where they could rest in safety. It would be a while before he would have the strength to change back and she knew from looking at him and her senses that he was muddled right now, overwhelmed by the changes he had undergone and his new instincts.

She would be there for him though.

She would take care of him.

And she would cling to the slender thread of hope that when he changed back, he would have the heart to forgive her for what she had done to him.

And he would take the one she would offer to him.

He would become her mate.

CHAPTER 15

Owen slowly opened his eyes and looked across to his left where Cait lay beside him, curled up on her side beneath a tattered black blanket. He recalled her bringing it back from one of her forays into what he presumed was the nearest town. It had been the second time she had donned his jeans and the black t-shirt and headed out of the cave.

The first time she had returned with meat for him, and he vaguely remembered growling at her and a sense that he had been angry. Not because she had left, but because he had feared she had done something awful in order to obtain the food.

She had reassured him that she had stolen it and he had taken what she had offered, carrying it off to his side of the cave to eat it, filled with a deep desire to keep her away from his food.

As the days had passed, he had grown stronger and had started to master his instincts, learning that she wasn't a threat and she wouldn't take his food from him. He had tried to shift back into his human form twice, but neither attempt had been successful.

Both had rendered him unconscious.

He had come around to find Cait scowling at him, her anger flowing around him in her sweet scent, but the tear tracks on her cheeks telling him that it was born of fear. He had worried her again.

He hadn't tried to shift in two full days.

Two days of Cait bringing him food and resting with him beneath the blanket.

Each time she returned, she would strip and change back into her cat form. She would bathe him, licking his fur, and he had done the same to her last night, cleaning her and paying close attention to her face.

She had made the reassuring noise at him again, the one that had given him strength countless times over the days since he had completed his first shift and had been stuck in his hellcat form.

He had come to love that noise.

It spoke of her affection for him, her tenderness and how she wanted to care for him.

Owen stretched beneath the covers, trying not to disturb her. He wanted to savour this moment in silence a little longer.

It felt good to be human again.

He raised his hands above his head and stared at his fingers. His nails were black and there was nothing he could do about it. He looked like a goth, but then it was a small price to pay for the incredible ability he had gained, and the strength that had come with it. It flowed through him, a buzz that made him want to leap out of bed and test the limits of his new body.

He would be faster too now, and his senses would be an advantage in any battle.

On top of all of that, he was now immortal.

Immortal.

He sighed and looked back at Cait, drinking in her beauty as she slept soundly, nestled close to him.

There was something else he was too.

He rolled onto his side and brushed the backs of his right fingers across her cheek. Her nose wrinkled up and she swatted at his hand. He smiled and persisted, not letting her deter him. He caressed her cheek and then swept his fingers over her temple, catching the long strands of her black hair and tucking it behind her ear, revealing the full depth of her beauty.

She murmured and tried to bat him away again.

"Cait," he whispered.

Her eyes shot open, locking straight onto his, her surprise rolling through him as his senses sharpened and fixed on her.

"Owen." She sat up and the blanket fell away from her bare chest.

He groaned and closed his eyes. "Cover yourself."

The rustle of material said she had done as he had requested, putting him out of his misery. He was strong enough to shift back, but he didn't think he was strong enough to get physical with her, and that was exactly what he would want to do if she sat around him in the nude.

"When did you shift?" Her fingers lightly brushed his brow. "Are you feeling okay?"

He nodded and opened his eyes, shifting them back to her. Hers widened again.

"Your eyes are green." She looked as if she hadn't expected that and he frowned. She shrugged. "They were blue in your cat form... I just thought..."

He could see why she would think he would have blue eyes now. Every hellcat he had met had blue ones.

"Maybe it's because I wasn't born one." He pushed himself up onto his elbow.

Cait dropped her eyes to her lap and frowned. "I'm sorry."

Owen sighed again, sat up and took hold of her left hand, clutching it in his and looking at it. He hadn't meant to make her feel guilty about what had happened, not when he knew she already felt terrible.

"It's strange… I won't deny that." He toyed with her fingers, looking at them to give her a moment to pull herself back together again. "I'll get used to it though, and I'm stronger now."

She kept her eyes on their hands, her sleek black hair falling down her chest as she held the blanket over it with her other hand.

"Can you still use magic?" she whispered to their hands.

He nodded even though she couldn't see it and then turned his hand over in hers and focused on it. Checking his magic had been the first thing he had done on successfully shifting back.

A slender blue rose appeared above his palm and he caught it, twisted his hand and offered it to her. She lifted her cerulean gaze to meet his, a flicker of relief shining in it that he felt inside her too. He loved how he could sense things about her now, could detect her emotions, and he wanted to ask about it but he was afraid it would push her too hard too soon. He didn't want to drive her away.

"I should have had more control." Cait lowered her gaze to the rose and took it from him, staring at it as she twirled the stem in her fingers. "Owen… I… the reason I bit you… it's… well…"

He hid his smile as she struggled with her words, her feelings in disarray, leaping between hopeful and afraid. He had intended to save this talk for later, asking her about the other difference he could feel in him, but it seemed she wanted it out there now.

No secrets between them.

He could live with that.

"I think…" She finally lifted her blue eyes back up to meet his and rushed out, "I think you're my mate."

He smiled this time and placed his hand around the one she held the blue rose in. "If you had told me that before I had gone through changing into a hellcat, I might have been shocked."

Her eyes widened. "You knew?"

He nodded. "There's something in your scent. Everything that I felt and that happened when I was in my cat form was muddled and confused, but when I shifted back, it all fell into place."

He drew her hand to him and pressed a long kiss to her fingers before looking deep into her eyes.

"I know you're my mate."

Tears lined her long dark lashes and she pulled her hand from his grip and turned her cheek to him, staring off to his right towards the mouth of the cave.

"It doesn't change what I did though, does it?" She closed her eyes and clutched the rose to her chest. "I bit you and I almost killed you… and now you're a hellcat and you didn't want to be one. I've changed your life—"

"Cait," Owen interjected before she could go any further and upset herself for no good reason. He moved onto his knees in front of her and took hold of both of her arms. He ran his hands down them to her hands and held them gently as he looked at her, seeing her fear and feeling every emotion she experienced coursing through his own blood. "Yes, you bit me... but it felt incredible."

She looked at him and opened her mouth to speak but snapped it shut again when he frowned at her.

"I admit I could have lived without the pain and the fever... and the threat of imminent death." He cursed himself when she looked away again, closing her eyes, causing a tear to slip onto her cheek. He wasn't doing a very good job of this. He should have rehearsed it before waking her because he had known how she would be, how she blamed herself for everything that had happened. He only wanted to take her pain away. "I can't say I ever wanted to be a hellcat because I never thought about it. It's not the sort of thing people think about happening to them... but I'm not angry that I am one now... I'm not upset that you changed me into one and made me like you... because—"

"I was coming back." She cut him off and swiftly turned to face him, dropping the rose and clutching both of his hands in hers. "I went to see the other female hellcat... Alice... in the fae town. She told me what to do. I was coming back to you and Marius darted me... and I should have done something different. I should have sensed him or been more aware of my surroundings."

But she hadn't been, because she had been afraid for him, rushing to save him and placing herself in danger because of it.

Because she loved him.

He could see it in her eyes.

She loved him and she feared he was going to leave her.

His little kitty had a lot to learn about him. He never walked away from anything.

"Can I speak now?" he said and her cheeks coloured.

He smiled and lifted her hands, luring them towards him. When she tried to release him, he caught her wrists and pulled her closer, refusing to let her get away from him. Another thing she had to learn about him. He never let his prey escape him, not once he had them in his sights.

And there was a part of her that he had in his crosshairs.

Her heart.

He was going to steal it from her just as she had stolen his.

"Look at me," he husked and she did as he asked, raising her blue eyes back to meet his green ones. His heart pounded but he breathed slowly, calming himself as he looked deep into her eyes, seeing his future in them.

His mate. His one true love. "I'm not upset about what happened, Cait. I'm not angry that you changed me into a hellcat, because you've been changing me since I met you and all of it has been for the better, and I'm sure this change will be too."

"I've been changing you?" Her brow crinkled and her eyes searched his.

Owen drew her closer and gathered her into his arms. He lifted her onto his lap, the feel of her bare backside on his thighs almost doing him in and wrecking his concentration at the vital moment when he needed to stay focused and keep on track.

He nodded and held her, his left arm around her waist, pinning her against him. Her hands clutched his bare shoulders, her rosy lips parting as she breathed, tempting him into looking at them. Another distraction. He wanted to kiss her, but first he had something he needed to tell her.

"You've made me stronger... able to face all my fears. You've made me braver... willing to share my secrets. You've made me weaker too... but in the best way." He smiled when she looked ready to point out there was no good way of being weak and pressed his finger to her lips to silence her. "You've made me weaker... dependent upon someone for the first time in what feels like forever... because my happiness depends on you being at my side, in my life."

Her breath hitched against his finger and her eyes grew enormous, and his heart raced in time with hers.

"But if you say you'll be mine... if you say you'll be with me forever... at my side where I need you most... then you will change that weakness into a strength, one that will live in my heart and will never fade and never die." He lifted his finger from her lips and cupped her cheek in his palm, his eyebrows furrowing as he stared deep into her eyes, seeing the warmth stirring in them as he felt the happiness flowing through her, the joy he had created with a handful of honest words from his heart to hers. "Say you'll be mine, Cait... say you love me as I love you."

She swallowed hard and threw her arms around his neck, her chest striking his with enough force to knock him backwards. He fell onto the hard ground of the cave with her on top of him, her legs astride his hips, and wrapped his arms around her as she smiled down at him, her blue eyes filled with fire.

"I will be yours, Owen Nightingale... because I love you too."

She dropped her head and captured his lips in a kiss that melted away all of his fears, leaving only happiness behind as he felt the depth of her feelings for him. They flowed through him, mingling with his own, a product of a bond she had begun in his home in the fae town when she had taken his blood and had completed here in the free realm when she had given her blood to him to save his life.

He rolled her over onto the blanket, settling himself between her thighs, and kissed her, pouring his feelings for her into it and losing himself in the moment.

Whatever the future held for him, he could face it, because Cait would be with him.

His mate.

He had been afraid to fall in love and allow anyone close to him, and now he had a mate.

She truly had bewitched him. His bad little kitty.

She leaned her head back to break the kiss and he drew away and looked down at her. Mischief coloured her blue eyes and he wondered what she was thinking. She played with the hair at the back of his head, pushing her fingers through it as she smiled up at him.

"You didn't finish your job."

He huffed. "I was indisposed."

She clucked her tongue. "Is that a fancy way of saying you didn't finish it? I think I finished it."

He brushed his fingers down her cheek and kissed the tip of her nose. "I helped."

Her nose wrinkled. "I guess… but I think you'll find I cut his head off."

"You did?" He grimaced when she nodded. He had missed that part and he was glad of it. He never had been fond of decapitation. There were cleaner methods of dispatching a foe. "I guess you can add 'good with swords' to your résumé then."

"I'm good with other weapons too… and I know Hell like the back of my hand and can use the portals freely. I'm also adventurous and like to travel." Her smile widened and he had the feeling this was turning into an impromptu interview. "So I have this money… and I might be interested in investing it in a business… provided I'm made into a partner."

"A partner?" He mock scowled. He liked the idea of having a partner, especially one with her abilities. It would be nice to have someone watching his back during the more dangerous jobs and she knew Hell well. "I'll take it under consideration."

She pouted and stroked his neck, sending a pleasant shiver down his spine. "What do I have to do to convince you to hire me?"

The wicked edge to her eyes said she already knew the answer to that question.

Nothing.

But he would take a bribe.

"Kiss me." He lowered his gaze to her mouth.

She smiled, rolled him onto his back and kissed him again, making him forget everything as her lips swept across his and her tongue stroked the seam of his lips. He groaned and let her in, tackling her tongue with his and clutching the back of her neck, holding her to him as he kissed her.

Her hands pressed to his bare chest and he burned where she touched him, on fire with a deep need for more of her.

A need that he felt sure would never die.

It would burn as hot and fierce as their love.

Born of two hearts that now beat as one.

A blue eternal flame.

The End

ABOUT THE AUTHOR

Felicity Heaton is a New York Times and USA Today best-selling author who writes passionate paranormal romance books. In her books she creates detailed worlds, twisting plots, mind-blowing action, intense emotion and heart-stopping romances with leading men that vary from dark deadly vampires to sexy shape-shifters and wicked werewolves, to sinful angels and hot demons!

If you're a fan of paranormal romance authors Lara Adrian, J R Ward, Sherrilyn Kenyon, Gena Showalter, Larissa Ione and Christine Feehan then you will enjoy her books too.

If you love your angels a little dark and wicked, the best-selling Her Angel series is for you. If you like strong, powerful, and dark vampires then try the Vampires Realm series or any of her stand-alone vampire romance books. If you're looking for vampire romances that are sinful, passionate and erotic then try the best-selling Vampire Erotic Theatre series. Or if you prefer huge detailed worlds filled with hot-blooded alpha males in every species, from elves to demons to dragons to shifters and angels, then take a look at the new Eternal Mates series.

If you have enjoyed this story, please take a moment to contact the author at **author@felicityheaton.co.uk** or to post a review of the book online

Connect with Felicity:
Website – http://www.felicityheaton.co.uk
Blog – http://www.felicityheaton.co.uk/blog/
Twitter – http://twitter.com/felicityheaton
Facebook – http://www.facebook.com/felicityheaton
Goodreads – http://www.goodreads.com/felicityheaton
Mailing List – http://www.felicityheaton.co.uk/newsletter.php

FIND OUT MORE ABOUT HER BOOKS AT:
http://www.felicityheaton.co.uk

Made in the USA
Middletown, DE
18 December 2018